Into The Labyrinth

Mage Errant Book 1

John Bierce

ISBN: 9781731550941

To my cat, because why not.

CHAPTER ONE

Hugh of Emblin

Hugh of Emblin wasn't good at much, but he was very, very good at hiding. Which was good, because he really needed to be.

"Where are you hiding, sheepherder? The longer it takes us to find you, the worse it will be for you!"

Hugh slid farther back into the space behind the bookshelf. Rhodes and his friends might have chosen him as their favorite victim, but their attention span usually wasn't too long. If he stayed hidden long enough, they'd eventually get bored and find something else to amuse themselves.

Hugh waited until the noise had faded, then slowly let himself relax- too soon, unfortunately. A hand reached in and grabbed his arm, then hauled him out into the library aisle. Hugh stumbled to his knees on the polished granite floor.

"Now, what are you doing in the library, sheepherder?" a voice asked.

Hugh took a deep breath and looked up. Rhodes Charax was smiling down at him, two of his lackeys grinning at his shoulders. Rhodes was everything Hugh wasn't— tall where Hugh was short, muscular where

4

Hugh was skinny, handsome where Hugh was forgettable, nobility where Hugh was the son of merchants, blue-eyed to Hugh's brown eyes, blonde to Hugh's dark hair, and a far, far better mage than Hugh had any hope of being. Even Rhodes' white uniform was clearly custom tailored to him, unlike Hugh's poorly fitting, off-white uniform from the academy's supplies.

"Everyone knows sheepherders can't read, so that can't be why you're here. Why are you here, sheepherder?"

"I'm not a sheepherder," Hugh said quietly. He could feel his face going red.

"What's that?" Rhodes said.

Hugh glared at him. "I'm not a sheepherder."

Rhodes kicked Hugh in the ribs, sending him sprawling.

"Didn't anyone ever tell you not to lie to your betters, sheepherder?" Rhodes said. "Though maybe if you were about to claim that you were one of the sheep I might believe you."

Rhodes' goons snickered at that. Hugh clenched his fists as he clambered to his knees again.

"You should stay on the ground where you belong, sheepherder." Rhodes lifted back his leg to kick Hugh again, but a voice intervened.

"I imagine that where he belongs is in class— the same as you three."

Rhodes and his friends spun around in alarm, and Hugh used that as an opportunity to scramble to his feet.

"It's our free period." Rhodes didn't even seem worried. Not that he had any reason to be concerned. He'd done worse in class without getting in trouble. It wasn't any surprise- Rhodes' family had immense political influence even hundreds of leagues outside their borders.

"Well, spend it somewhere else." The mysterious voice sounded unamused. Hugh couldn't get a look at the man yet past the bullies. "You're not exactly using the library for its intended purpose."

Rhodes shot Hugh a look that promised this wasn't over yet, but strode off with the others. They all burst into laughter while still in earshot. Hugh winced. Rhodes was always worse for days after the rare occasions a teacher or other mage interfered.

The librarian that the mysterious voice belonged to studied him. He was tall and wiry, with a scruffy head of brown hair that looked like it hadn't seen a comb in days. He couldn't be much more than twice Hugh's fifteen years.

After a few moments of silence, the librarian sighed. "What's your name?"

"Hugh." Hugh looked away from the librarian, hoping that he would move on so that Hugh could find somewhere to be alone.

"Just Hugh?"

"People call me Hugh of Emblin, sir. To distinguish me from the other Hughs here."

The librarian gave him a curious glance. Hugh could already feel the usual questions coming. Mages weren't ever born in Emblin, and yet Hugh had been. Not that he'd ever amount to much of a mage. But, to his surprise, the librarian didn't ask him about being from Emblin.

"Would you like me to report those other students to your instructors?" the librarian said.

Hugh gaped at him in surprise for a moment. The librarian waited patiently. After a few moments, Hugh collected himself.

"Wouldn't do any good, sir," Hugh said.

The librarian cocked an eyebrow at him. "Wouldn't do any good?"

Hugh just stared at the ground, waiting until he could leave. Eventually, however, he realized the librarian was ready to wait all day for an answer.

"That was Rhodes Charax, sir."

The librarian just gave him the same level gaze.

"Rhodes' uncle is the king of Highvale, sir. Not to mention he's the most promising mage in our year. All the teachers just stand to gain by staying on his good side. I'm just a nobody, though. None of them are going to stick their heads out for me."

The librarian seemed to consider that for a while, then sighed. "Very well." He started to walk away, then turned back towards Hugh. "Next time, try hiding in the stacks instead of the main law section. Much better hiding spots, plus the reading material is much more interesting." He looked like he wanted to say more, but turned and left.

Hugh sighed. He'd gotten off easy this time, at least. And the tip about the stacks wasn't a bad one.

Hugh, thankfully enough, didn't run into Rhodes and his lackeys on the way to his next class. That didn't make him feel much better, however. His next class was Basics of Unattuned Spellcasting- or, as everyone called it, Cantrips. It was supposed to be one of the easiest classes for first years like himself who hadn't attuned yet, but was yet another reason why life at Skyhold had been such a nightmare for him. For anyone else, it should have been a dream come true- being sent to study at the Academy at Skyhold, one of the most prestigious mage schools on the entire continent at Ithos.

Anyone else wasn't Hugh.

Hugh slipped into a desk at the back of the class, where he was less likely to draw attention. The students that didn't participate in Rhodes' harassment of Hugh didn't care about his presence, so he really just wanted to avoid the teacher's attention. Unfortunately, the eager young woman teaching today almost immediately noticed him.

There hadn't been enough full mages that wanted to teach first year classes this year, so Hugh's class had been stuck with a rotating population of journeyman mages. He didn't know this one's name, but it didn't matter. Every new journeyman thought they could be the one to solve the infamous Hugh of Emblin's problems, and in the end they were all proved wrong.

Today they were supposed to be learning a spell to set a stick on fire- about as basic as it came. Hugh paid careful attention to the teacher's description of how they should channel their mana, even though he already knew what she was going to say. He'd been in the library to read about this spell ahead of class, desperately hoping he could get a spell right for once. It had been on his way back that Rhodes had found him.

Hugh took a deep breath and focused on the stick he held. Some of the other students were having a little trouble, but most already had their sticks at least smoking. He visualized the forms perfectly, and channeled his mana just so. He could tell that the teacher, as well as a number of his classmates, were already watching him to see how he would mess things up this time.

"Once you all have figured out setting the sticks on fire, we'll move onto controlling the intensity of the flame, and maybe even to changing their colors."

Hugh's stick exploded with magical light, then abruptly went dark again. He tried to shut his eyes in time, but his vision remained filled with spots.

The stick wasn't even charred.

"You're a menace, sheepherder," someone nearby whispered. Several other students were muttering and complaining as well.

"I'm not a sheepherder," Hugh muttered.

"Everyone's bound to mess up sometimes. Give it another try, Hugh," the teacher said.

Hugh blinked away the last of the spots from his eyes and looked around. Everyone was staring at him now.

"How's he going to screw it up this time?" someone else whispered.

Hugh swallowed angrily and focused on the stick again. First, visualize the spellforms- the invisible geometric diagrams you were supposed to envision to cast a spell. He'd spent a solid hour memorizing them. He knew them inside and out. Next, channel the mana. You couldn't push your mana into the forms- mana flowed like water, and pushing it would do about as much good as pushing on a stream. The geometric designs you were supposed to envision helped you guide mana's flow.

The mana flowed perfectly into the forms, at exactly the right speed. It flowed precisely where it should. And nothing happened. No- something was happening.

A small handful of dim sparks fell from the stick and vanished before hitting the desk.

"Come now, Hugh, you can do it. Let's try again," the teacher said. The whole class was still whispering to themselves and watching him with amusement. He couldn't blame them- he had to be the most incompetent mage to ever arrive at Skyhold.

Hugh took a shaky breath, then focused on the stick again. Visualize your forms. Channel your mana. Visualize your forms. Channel your mana. Visualize your forms. Channel your…

The stick jerked out of his hand and smacked him in the forehead. The whole class burst into laughter.

The teacher made Hugh try six more times in front of the class before she finally gave up. She hadn't done it to be cruel to Hugh- she was genuinely trying to help him. That didn't make Hugh feel any better disposed towards her, or to the classmates who found him a topic of pity at best, amusement or even scorn far more often.

Eventually she'd had to move on. Hugh just sat in the back of the class staring at his desk, not even trying to pay attention. When class got out, he trudged out of class near the back of the pack. Everyone else was chattering excitedly on their way to dinner, but he barely looked up past his feet. The teacher called out to him, but he pretended not to hear her over the sound of his classmates.

He arrived to dinner late, and had quite a wait in line before he managed to get his food. It was fish and potatoes again tonight. Some of the other students complained, but Hugh didn't mind- the meal reminded him of home. Potatoes and fish were two of the things that Emblin had plenty of- the others being timber and sheep.

Hugh sat at a bench by himself, hoping desperately that no one would try to sit near him or talk to him. Thankfully, no one did. He spotted Rhodes across the dining hall sitting with his lackeys and a couple of girls. Rhodes noticed him back and said something to his table that made them all laugh, but didn't do anything else.

Most of the meal went by in a sullen funk, Hugh

slowly picking at his food. Towards the end of the meal, though, he overheard something made him pay attention.

"...Dragonslayer is going to be there!" one of the students at the table behind him said.

Hugh perked up. Could they mean...

"No way," a second student said. "Aedan Dragonslayer hasn't taken an apprentice in years."

"I overheard two teachers talking about it," the first student said. "He's picking a new apprentice this year."

Hugh turned around to listen at this point.

"Who do you think he'll pick?" another student said.

One of the students, a hanger-on of Rhodes', noting Hugh watching, grinned maliciously. "Maybe he's planning to pick Hugh." The table burst into laughter. Hugh flushed, and turned back to his food.

"He might have slain dragons, but teaching Hugh might be a task too challenging for even him." The table burst out laughing again, and Hugh stood up abruptly. He grabbed his plate and brought it to the scullery window, then stalked out the door. Rhodes, thankfully, had already left dinner.

As Hugh trudged back to his room, he sank even deeper into his funk. They had just a few short weeks before the Choosing. Every year, hundreds of mages looked over the students, choosing one or two as apprentices. Every student got picked by someone, but not all mages were equal. Most students were picked by a fairly average, run of the mill mage- one whose contributions to Skyhold weren't great enough that they could get away with not taking on apprentices. The more prestigious a mage was, the earlier they got to choose their apprentices- Aedan Dragonslayer, as one of the most famous mages alive, had likely already chosen his apprentice weeks ago, though it wouldn't be announced until the Choosing ceremony. A great many of the students were taken on by various working mage groups within Skyhold- the cleaning staff always needed mages to help take care of things like alchemical reagent spills, for instance.

Hugh doubted anyone was going to Choose him. He'd just keep waiting and waiting, until he was all by himself in the Great Hall. Maybe, if he was lucky, he'd get picked by the cleaning mages.

Lost in his own thoughts, he didn't notice that his door was open until he reached out to open it. Inside, his room was a complete disaster area. His uniforms had been trampled, his blankets ripped. Someone had pissed on his mattress. His books were lying on the ground, pages bent, and his sling- one of his only mementos of Emblin- had been cut to pieces.

Hugh stood in shock. Rhodes and his friends had been relentless before, but they'd always left his room alone. His room had been locked, and just about the only magics that Hugh was actually capable of were wards- his room had been well defended, for a first year student. Rhodes and his friends shouldn't have been able to break through them- wardbreaking wasn't even taught until second year. Rhodes must have convinced a teacher to privately tutor him on the topic.

If he didn't even have the privacy of his own room, Hugh felt like he'd go insane. He had nothing else. He didn't have any friends. No one from Emblin ever wrote him, ashamed that a family of good Emblin stock should have a mage in it. He'd been rushed off to Skyhold almost the instant his mage gifts became apparent. It was worth it to his family to hide their shame. Not that they'd ever had any pride in him in the first place.

Hugh slammed his door shut, slid down to the floor, and then buried his head between his knees to cry.

CHAPTER TWO

The Choosing

After he stopped crying, Hugh wandered the halls in a daze for hours. Whenever he heard or saw someone, he turned down a different hallway. He even avoided the guards. Eventually, though, he found himself somewhere familiar- the library.

The glowing crystals that lit the halls and library gave off light constantly, so he had no trouble seeing. He avoided the main sections of the library, since there would likely still be people there even at this hour, and headed into the stacks.

The librarian had definitely been right about the number of hiding spots. The rest of the library levels accessible to first year students were all built into neatly laid out tunnels. The stacks, however, looked like they'd been an afterthought, crammed into a jumbled mess of disorganized rooms and tunnels, with overcrowded shelves and even study desks piled with books. He found an aisle that had been blocked off by another shelf, forming a hidden hallway. He found another room filled with wooden crates of old textbooks, where he could easily hide.

Best of all, however, he found an almost entirely empty room forgotten behind a row of shelves whose books hadn't been touched for so long they were covered in dust. It even had a door that opened inwards into the room- which was for the best, as otherwise the shelf wouldn't have let the door open. There were a few empty shelves, a pile of old textbooks, and a desk in the room. Most amazing of all- there was a window.

The glass of the window was old and discolored, the frame warped and old, but Hugh still managed to force it open. He found himself looking westwards into the night, out over the immense sea of sand known as the Endless Erg. He'd sailed over the Endless Erg on the last leg of his voyage to Skyhold on one of the great sandships. While it wasn't actually endless, it was immense, and far too dangerous to cross on foot. If the blistering heat during the day didn't get you, the icy nights would, or the lack of water, or the horrifying monsters. The wind was blowing particularly coldly tonight, given how close it was to midwinter.

When Hugh looked down, he could see the sandship port far below him. As he looked around, he could see more of Skyhold itself. Skyhold was carved into the sides of a massive mountain that split into two peaks near the top. The mountain was riddled with tunnels and towers. Keeps, balconies, and other structures rose from the sides, built into the mountain itself. Tens of thousands of people lived in Skyhold, though no one had an exact count. There were nearly three thousand students at the academy alone- nearly a third of which were in their first year.

Hugh must have spent hours just gazing out of the window. He'd seen very little of the outside over the last few months- none of the classrooms or student rooms had windows, and many days he'd been too busy to find a window or balcony. Hugh couldn't remember the last time he'd actually gone outside. When he finally pulled himself away from the window and shut it, a plan had already taken shape in his mind.

Over the next few hours, Hugh carefully smuggled his possessions into the hidden library room. He salvaged the clothes and blankets he could- Rhodes and his friends had clearly been in a hurry when they ransacked his room, because the damage was much less bad than he'd originally thought. There was no way Hugh could sneak his mattress into the little room even if he wanted to, but he'd be fine sleeping in a nest of blankets for now. His books and other personal items easily fit on the desk and shelf. There wasn't a chair for the desk, but he managed to- with considerable difficulty- drag one from the stacks into the little room. The very last thing he did was craft new wards for his room.

It was well into the early hours of the morning when Hugh finished, and he fell asleep the instant he curled up into his blankets. He didn't dream at all.

Hugh missed his morning classes, but he wasn't overly broken up about it. There was a field trip outside to some of Skyhold's magic defenses today in Mana Theory class, so he wouldn't be missed. By the afternoon, he felt ready to head to class. Thankfully, he managed to pass the day without incident- even the new Cantrips teacher decided to leave him alone after yesterday's failures.

Over the next few days, Hugh fell into a new pattern. He scrounged the stacks for old sacks, discarded papers, and the like, eventually managing to construct a crude but comfortable mattress. The ruined school uniforms were surprisingly easy to get replacements for- students were expected to ruin quite a few uniforms while learning magic.

The stacks had their own bathrooms. They weren't as nice as the restrooms in the student halls, but they still had the same running water (a luxury that Hugh hadn't known back in Emblin), and even if there weren't showers, he could still get clean enough using rags and the sinks.

Even with how well hidden his new lair was, Hugh wasn't completely comfortable with his current wards. His old wards had proven insufficient to protect his old room, but living in a library had its perks. He managed to find an old book on wards that had been misshelved in the stacks- only the most basic introductory spellbooks and magic theory texts were supposed to be shelved in the public access areas of the library, but this book looked to have been misplaced for decades. It was at least a century old, and even though its wards were archaic and old fashioned, they were a lot more effective than anything he'd had access to so far.

Hugh didn't dare bring lamps into the library, and the room didn't have glow crystals of its own- but basic light spells were the only other type of magic he felt comfortable with other than warding. It had still taken him much longer to learn them than normal- his early light spells kept shining far too brightly and blinding him- but he'd eventually mastered them, much to his (and his teacher's) surprise.

Hugh had never been much of a huge reader back in Emblin- they'd only ever had a few books. Even then, Hugh did his absolute best to stay out of his family's way, so he really hadn't had the chance to read much, preferring to wander around the woods instead.

Here at Skyhold, he'd taken to reading with a vengeance. It had been his only real escape from his misery. Now that he was living in the library, he found himself reading far more than ever. He devoured books on history, botany, and astronomy. He read through countless bestiaries describing magical beasts- finding, to his amusement, that it was extremely common for any two bestiaries to radically disagree on the basic details of monsters.

Hugh also spent quite a lot of time watching the librarians' origami golems. Many of the librarians were paper mages, and crafted folded paper golems to accomplish a wide array of tasks. Paper cranes and miniature paper dragons were folded up messages that would unfold themselves upon reaching the receiver of the message. Knee high paper monkeys were regularly sent down into the stacks to retrieve books. Hugh helped more than a few of them retrieve a difficult book from the stack shelves.

Surprisingly, none of the faculty seemed to notice his disappearance from his dormitory room. Or maybe it wasn't surprising, given how little they expected from him.

While his teachers didn't seem to notice or care, Hugh constantly worried about the librarians. He was very careful to plan out his routes and move very cautiously through the stacks during the day, to make sure he ran into as few librarians as possible. None of them seemed to pay him much attention- the library was immense, and the publicly accessible stacks alone would have been the size of a small fortress if they had been built outside the mountain. Hugh was hardly the first student to evade bullies by hiding in the stacks- though he doubted that actually living in them was particularly common.

He ran into the librarian who had rescued him from Rhodes several times over the next few weeks. The librarian never approached him, but he often gave Hugh odd looks. Hugh hadn't noticed it before, but the librarian's uniform was very different than most librarians- instead of the short, light grey coats that most librarians wore, his coat reached down to his knees and had red trim. Hughes had no idea what that meant. The librarian also always seemed to have a satchel overstuffed with books and scrolls at his side.

Rhodes definitely did notice Hugh's absence from the student dormitories, on the other hand. Hugh frequently found himself having to spend long periods evading Rhodes to keep him from following into the library. He even started eating in another cafeteria- one out of favor with the students for its distance from the dorms and the large number of journeyman mages and librarians who ate there. Hugh didn't mind any of that.

Rhodes, spoiled of much of his fun, began stepping up his harassment campaign even more when he had the chance. Hugh rarely had a day where he wasn't tripped in the hall or zapped with whatever new cantrip Rhodes and his lackeys had learned in class.

Still, life was much better than it had been for a while. Hugh couldn't say he was happy, but it was bearable.

The day of the Choosing came at Midwinter, just under a month after Hugh had moved into his little library room. His classmates had talked about nothing else for weeks- even Rhodes stopped paying much attention to Hughes as the day drew closer. People gossiped constantly about what master they'd pick if they got to choose (Aedan Dragonslayer was the current favorite) and what sort of mage they'd like to become.

Mages wandered up and down the halls constantly, talking to various students, watching classes, and otherwise making a nuisance of themselves. With all the chaos, most teachers largely gave up on trying to get much teaching done.

The actual process of the Choosing was considerably less chaotic than it seemed, however. Mages didn't have to wade through the entire listings of potential first year candidates to find an apprentice- they only needed to look through the list of candidates with appropriate affinities.

Everyone had their own affinities- types of magic that it was easier to perform. The mana that everyone channeled from the Aether around them was identical, but it got converted in the body to different types. A mage with an affinity for fire could more easily convert aetheric mana to fire mana, a mage with an affinity for plants could more easily convert aetheric mana to plant mana, and so on and so forth. There were hundreds of known affinities, and many of them overlapped considerably with one another. To make it even more confusing, many mages had overlapping affinities- a mage with affinities for fire and earth, for instance, could probably train a mage with a magma affinity.

You didn't necessarily have to train in a style of magic that matches your affinity, but it was much, much harder to train a different affinity. Many mages, in fact, couldn't accomplish it at all. And, once you'd trained enough with a type of mana, you became attuned to it, and it became much harder to attune to other styles of magic. Few mages successfully attuned to more than two types of mana, and many stuck to just one. There were a few unusual mages out there with three or more natural affinities, but they were very, very rare. Rhodes, unfortunately, was one of them.

That was Hugh's second big problem. He didn't seem to have an affinity. If he'd been a competent enough mage to start with, maybe that could have been a plus for him- any full mage could have probably taken him on as an apprentice. It would have been much more work to attune, and Hugh doubted he could have acquired more than a single attunement, but it would likely have been doable. Combined with his complete failure to be able to work magic, however? Hugh honestly doubted whether any mages would want to take him on. Maybe the janitorial mages- you just needed to be able to channel mana into devices to work with them.

So as the date of the Choosing had approached, nearly everyone but Hugh got more and more excited, while he grew more and more anxious. And now it was here, and Hugh had seldom been so miserable.

Hugh could barely make himself listen to Headmaster Tarik's speech. Normally he would have been riveted to every word she said- Tarik had been one of the mightiest stone mages on the continent in her prime, and was said to have singlehandedly raised a fortress in a week during one of the Havath Dominion's wars of expansion, stopping them in their tracks. Today, though, Hugh could only miserably imagine everyone else getting chosen, then being left unwanted by himself in the cavernous Great Hall.

Tarik eventually stepped away from the raised dais onstage, which was enchanted to project the speaker's words across the Great Hall. As she stepped off, the first mage to take an apprentice stepped onto the dais- Aedan Dragonslayer.

Mages got to choose their apprentices in order of prestige, and there was no-one more prestigious at all of Skyhold than Aedan Dragonslayer. He'd earned his name while still a journeyman, single-handedly slaying a rampaging ancient frost wyrm in his homeland of Tsarnassus. Since then he'd slain at least a dozen full grown dragons, two more ancient wyrms, and countless drakes, wyverns, and other draconic relatives. While draconic foes were his specialty, he had fought more than his share of other monsters as well- most notably an enormous hydra lurking in a ruined Ithonian city in the heart of an impassible jungle. Stories of his deeds were even told by the magic-hating people of Emblin.

The key to Aedan's success? He had no less than five attunements. The students weren't exactly sure what they all were, but it was known that he could fly and hurl lighting at the very least, and there were countless other rumors. One of the more ridiculous but tenacious rumors claimed that he could turn into a dragon himself.

Hugh would be lying if he claimed he had never dreamt about apprenticing to Aedan Dragonslayer. His mana reservoirs were considerable in size for his age, even if he didn't have anything else going for him. Realistically, though, Hugh had never imagined them to be more than just dreams- his inability to cast most spells, mixed with his lack of an affinity? He'd never be able to be a combat mage.

Aedan spent at least a minute staring out over the crowd sternly. Any other wizard would be expected to immediately announce their new apprentice, but the grey-haired, battlescarred mage could likely get away with

standing there however long he wanted. The entire
audience was silent and tensely awaiting Aedan to speak-
even the other full mages. Finally he opened his mouth.

"Rhodes Charax of Highvale," he said, then simply
stepped off the dais.

Hugh's heart plummeted into his stomach. He'd never
seriously expected to be chosen by Aedan, but for Rhodes
to be chosen instead? Hugh was ready to slink out of the
Great Hall then and there.

The rest of the students didn't agree, however.
Rhodes' many friends, admirers, and lackeys all applauded
fiercely. Rhodes himself looked absolutely triumphant as
he got up to meet Aedan by the side of the stage to begin
his apprenticeship.

Hugh could barely make himself pay attention for the
rest of the Choosing. He did note a few of the more
interesting selections, however. Sulassa Tidecaller, a water
mage who had once redirected an entire river to put out a
forest fire, chose a pair of twins- a boy and a girl- who had
blue eyes and hair that changed shades like the surface of
the sea. Artur Wallbreaker, a seven foot tall, muscle-bound
metal and stone attuned mage that carried a hammer that
must have weighed more than Hugh, chose a youth that
was clearly his son, and looked like he'd end up even
bigger than his father.

For the most part, Hugh just sunk further and further
into his own misery. The Choosing took most of the day to
finish, and Hugh just stayed seated as more and more
students left. Soon enough a quarter of the hall had
emptied, then half, then three quarters. There weren't a lot
of mages left to pick apprentices before the various work
groups started picking theirs. At this point, all Hugh hoped
for was to not be picked by the janitorial mages.

Hugh was feeling almost ready to burst into tears at this point. Not, of course, that many of the other mage students left looked too happy- there was no glory in getting chosen by a work group. Everyone dreamed about being apprenticed to a master, not just sitting in more large classes for several more years. There were just a few individual masters left, and…

"Hugh of Emblin."

CHAPTER THREE

Master

Hugh whipped his eyes back to the dais, convinced he'd misheard. On the dais was standing the last person Hugh would have expected- the librarian who had saved him from Rhodes and told him about the stacks. He felt a brief moment of hope, then saw two other students walking towards the stage, and his heart sank. Masters almost never took more than two apprentices.

Then the librarian looked right at him, and repeated himself clearly.

"Hugh of Emblin."

In a daze, Hugh got off the bench and stumbled towards the stage. Hugh had been chosen! He hadn't been abandoned in the Hall on his own after all. He didn't even know his new master's name or affinities, but he felt more relief than he'd ever felt since his magic first manifested.

As he walked closer, however, doubts had already started to flood his brain. His new master must just be representing the library work group... except Hugh could see the head librarians and his assistants still waiting to announce their selections. It must just be pity, then- the librarian had seen Hugh bullied, and then he must have looked at Hugh's records and seen how incompetent Hugh was. By the time he reached the stage, he was absolutely convinced of it.

Hugh was, to his own shame, absolutely fine with getting a master out of pity.

His new master looked at Hugh and his other two new apprentices as he stepped off stage, then simply gestured for them to follow him. The tall, slender mage walked at a pace that Hugh had to struggle to keep up with. As they strode out of the Great Hall, Hugh took the opportunity to study the other two apprentices, whose names he hadn't caught. It was no surprise that he hadn't met them before, given that there were over a thousand first year mages.

The first girl was taller than Hugh by several inches. She had the dark skin and long pale hair- closer to white than blonde- of one of the residents of the southwestern coast cities. The girl also had what looked like thin, treebranch shaped burn scars on her hands and one cheek. She had absolutely no expression on her face, and kept her eyes straight ahead.

The other apprentice was even shorter than Hugh. She was pale, with a brilliant shock of long red hair. She also had more tattoos than anyone he'd ever met before. The tattoos were interlocking geometric designs done in a brilliant blue- it almost looked like someone had tattooed spellforms all over her. They ran down her arms to her fingers, up her neck, and even onto her forehead and cheeks, though not onto the rest of her face. Hugh had never seen anyone like her, and hadn't the slightest clue where she was from. As he eyed her, she noticed him looking and gave him a furious glare in response. Hugh looked away quickly rather than maintain eye contact.

After a minute or two, Hugh finally worked up the nerve to speak to his new master, albeit barely above a whisper. "Sir… I'm, uh… I'm afraid I didn't catch your name."

The red-haired girl spoke up scornfully. "You didn't even catch your own name the first time, so no wonder."

Hugh winced.

The librarian turned around to face them, but didn't slow down at all. If Hugh had tried to walk backwards at even half that speed he would have immediately fallen down. The gangly mage gestured at himself. "My apologies- this is my first time taking apprentices, so I'm quite new to all this myself."

That hardly inspired Hugh's confidence.

"I am Alustin Haber, Librarian Errant," he said. Alustin- while still walking backwards and seemingly without looking- stepped to his left to avoid running into an incredibly overweight mage and his two new apprentices. "In case you didn't catch each other's names, this young gentleman here is Hugh of Emblin, the tall young woman here is Sabae Kaen Das, and our heavily tattooed friend is Talia of Clan Castis. Without waiting for a response, Alustin whirled back around.

The short redhead- Talia- glared at him. "I'm not your friend," she whispered.

Hugh looked away from her. Sabae was still just staring forwards, her face set in stone.

They group walked in silence for a few more minutes. Hugh had just realized that they were heading for the library when Sabae finally spoke up, loud and clear.

"Master Alustin, what's a Librarian Errant?"

Without slowing down, Alustin whirled around to face them again. "Excellent question, Sabae! A Librarian Errant is a mage who is sent out of Skyhold to retrieve books- grimoires stolen from our collection, tomes hidden away in the trapped and cursed lairs of long dead magicians, badly overdue textbooks, that sort of thing." Alustin turned back around and continued walking.

Hugh blinked in surprise, then lowered his gaze back to his feet. That... that actually sounded somewhat exciting. Much more so than he'd expected. He hadn't expected Alustin to be a battle mage. But... why would a mage like that want an apprentice like Hugh?

No one spoke again until they had reached the library, and even then it was just Alustin greeting other librarians, all of whom seemed quite pleased to see him, and gave the new apprentices plenty of curious looks.

Alustin's office was far into the librarian-only portions of the library. Alustin stopped at an unlabeled door that looked like it opened onto a broom closet, but when he unlocked it, revealed a shockingly spacious office- mages could likely hold combat practice in here, except for the low ceiling. Alustin didn't hit his head against it, but it certainly wouldn't be safe for him to jump.

"Come in, come in, don't be shy!" Alustin said.

The walls were lined with overloaded shelves and huge chalkboards inscribed with cramped handwriting, complex diagrams and spellforms, and a number of surprisingly good drawings. After a moment, Hugh realized that the floor was a huge chalkboard as well.

In the back was a massive desk that looked like it had

belonged to an old headmaster or even a king, but was at least a century past its prime, covered in chips, gouges, and even a few splinters. Hugh was sure there was absolutely no way the desk could fit through the door, and definitely not down the narrow wrought-iron spiral staircase leading upwards in one corner of the room. The desk was piled with countless books, scrolls, and sheafs of paper. Hugh wasn't even sure there was room to work. Instead of the normal wooden chairs you'd expect, there was an absolutely immense leather armchair behind the desk. Even the tall Librarian Errant would be dwarfed in it. Like the desk, it was well on its way to the garbage heap. In front of the desk were three equally battered but comfy-looking armchairs.

Alustin strode over to his desk. The apprentices moved to follow, but Talia abruptly came to a halt halfway across the room. Hugh and Sabae drifted to a halt behind her, confused.

"What in the all the thousand hells do you want with an absolutely useless mage?" Talia said. She seemed even angrier than before.

Hugh felt his face heat up. That's why she'd been so angry. She knew Hugh's reputation, and was insulted that he was tagging along with them. He snuck a glance at Sabae, and saw that she was staring off to the side, and looked more stone faced than ever. She couldn't even look at him, she was so embarrassed to be lumped in with him. He…

"You're not useless, Talia," Alustin said.

…What?

"Don't you go telling me it's snowing at midsummer, librarian. Not a one of my clan could make anything of me, or any of the tutors they found," Talia said. "I should have been a proper warmage like my parents and brothers, and instead I'm just a useless mess. I should warn you, though- I might not have any future as a battle mage, but I'm not letting you turn me into some paper shuffler who never sees the light of day. I won't let you pity me, either."

Hugh didn't have the slightest clue what was going on. Talia was... talking about herself? Then why was Sabae...?

Alustin watched Talia calmly throughout her outburst.

"You're not useless, Talia." Alustin looked at Sabae, then at Hugh. "None of you are useless. None of you have failed as mages. The Academy has failed all of you. You were expected to simply conform to the same curriculum as everyone else, but magic isn't that rigid."

"What sort of nonse...", Talia said.

Alustin talked right over her. "I didn't pick you out of pity, or because I wanted extra hands to sort through papers. I picked the three of you because I think you have potential, because I think you could become great mages."

Talia looked nearly as dumbstruck as Hugh felt. Even Sabae finally had an expression on her face as she gave Alustin a sharp look. Alustin was... he was...

Alustin was crazy.

Hugh couldn't keep his mouth shut anymore. "Every single teacher that's tried to teach me has given me up as a failure. I'm no real mage, I'm... I'm just some sort of freak."

Alustin gave him a flat look. "It's best not to trust what everyone knows, Hugh." Alustin shuffled a pile of papers on his desk. "Everyone said I'd never succeed as a battle mage, and I proved them all wrong."

Hugh shut his mouth.

Alustin actually looked a little angry now. "Skyhold

28

has begun to treat students as though they were interchangeable, as though there was only a single way to teach magic. They keep increasing class sizes and expecting everyone to learn identical spells from a book." He leaned forwards. "Magic doesn't work like that. There are countless paths of magic, and when the Academy runs across one that deviates too far from their norm? They've become entirely unable to handle it."

Alustin took a deep breath and seemed to calm down. "I meant to wait until later to discuss this with each of you individually, but it seems that we should get this over with now. Each of you has falsely been led to believe themselves useless as a mage. I intend to prove otherwise."

Alustin sat behind his desk, then gestured to the chairs in front of his desk. "Sit."

No one moved for a second. Sabae, interestingly, was the first to move. Hugh quickly followed her, and Talia hesitated for a moment, then claimed the third armchair. As Hugh settled in, he found that the armchair might be hideous, but was absurdly comfortable.

"It's not my place to tell your stories to each other," Alustin said, "and, in fact, I only know bits and pieces of them, despite extensive research. I highly encourage you to share your stories with each other, but I won't require it. I will, however, be telling you about each others' magical problems."

Hugh felt himself start to redden. He'd thought that...

"I don't do this to shame or embarrass any of you. In order to work together, mages must understand one another. Over the next few years the three of you will be working together constantly. Understand?"

Sabae nodded curtly. Hugh hesitantly nodded himself, and even Talia eventually grunted.

Alustin took a deep breath. "Talia here was born to a line of powerful fire mages. Her family was so confident she'd be another that they gave her flame-enhancing spellform tattoos before her affinities had even manifested. Unfortunately, Talia isn't a fire mage. Her affinities lie incredibly strongly in bone and dream- both rare and powerful affinities. Her tattoos, however, have inhibited her abilities to control her gifts- they force her into trying to control her affinities as though they were both fire, which has resulted in at least one destroyed classroom."

Hugh glanced at Talia, who promptly shot him back a challenging glare, as if daring him to say something. He looked away quickly. Her problem sounded awful, but at least she had affinities. Maybe there was some way to remove her tattoos?

"Sabae was also born into a powerful lineage of mages- storm mages each possessed of triple lightning, wind, and water affinities. Sabae, however, seems to completely lack the ability to control her powers more than a few inches away from her body. For many mages, that might not be a problem, but storm mages don't do anything up close. Sabae, unusually, was also born with a fourth affinit…"

At this point Sabae gave Alustin a direct glare. "No."

"I wasn't going to share your story, Sabae, merely your…."

"That is part of my story, Master Alustin."

Alustin stared at her for a moment, then sighed. "Very well. The two of us will speak of this later."

Hugh was a bit shocked. Double affinities were quite common. Many mages who lacked a second affinity still developed a second attunement- it was much more work without a natural affinity, but still worthwhile. Triple affinities, however, were extremely rare. And Sabae apparently had four affinities. Even with her apparent personal setbacks, that was absurd. The only mage he'd heard of with more was Aedan Dragonslayer, with five.

That, of course, reminded him of Rhodes. How many affinities must Rhodes have in order for Aedan to have chosen him as a student? There's no way that even being royalty would have impressed Aedan enough on its own.

"Last, but not least, we have Hugh."

Hugh jumped a little in his seat, then reddened. The other two both had fixable problems. Whatever Alustin claimed, Hugh was just…

"Hugh's problems managed to go undiagnosed by any of his teachers for some time. I only figured them out myself after several weeks of research. I was curious about him after the first time we met. Hugh here, as you might have heard earlier, is from Emblin."

At this point Talia interrupted. "Everyone knows that no mages come from Emblin. It's just a bunch of sheepherders."

Hugh looked away from the others. "I'm not a sheepherder," he muttered.

"I believe I said something about things that everyone knows, Talia."

There was a pause, then Talia made a grunting noise. Alustin apparently decided that was enough of an apology for interrupting and moved on.

"It is true that very few mages come from Emblin, but it's not due to any particular trait of the people that live there. Emblin is, in fact, one of the deepest mana deserts on the entire continent of Ithos."

31

Hugh looked back at Alustin. "Emblin's not a desert, sir. It's mostly forests and mountains." Alustin gave him an odd look, and Hugh quickly looked away.

"A mana desert, Hugh, not a regular desert."

"What is it, Master Alustin?" Sabae asked.

"A mana desert… did they teach you nothing of the flow of the Aether in your classes yet?"

No one said anything. Alustin sighed. "That's an entire lecture all of its own. For now, let's just say that Emblin has very, very little mana available to use. Even fully trained mages must struggle to channel any mana from the Aether there, which is why they visit there so seldom. A new, untrained mage in Emblin would essentially be unable to channel any mana at all. Emblin likely has as many potential mages as any other nation, they merely never learn to use their abilities."

Hugh hadn't ever heard anything like this about Emblin before. Everyone back home said that the reason there were no mages there was because they'd driven them all out in the centuries after the fall of the Ithonian Empire.

"Hugh, if he'd been any weaker, never would have manifested any abilities at all. He was, however, born with an astonishingly powerful talent- at only fifteen, his mana reserves are as large as those of many fully trained mages. As he gets older and farther along in his training, they will only grow even further."

Hugh had what now?

"And, in order to begin manifesting any magic whatsoever, his system was forced to strain much, much harder to channel mana. This is why you have so much trouble with cantrips, Hugh- your body is trying to flood every spell you perform with far too much mana."

Hugh blinked. "Too much mana, sir? All this time, it's

just been a matter of too much mana?" His mouth worked silently for a moment, then he started laughing. It wasn't a happy laugh at all. It was either laugh or scream.

After a couple minutes, Hugh finally calmed down a little bit. Talia and Sabae were both staring at him oddly, while Alustin just looked patient.

"Not just that, no. If that had been it I would have just alerted your teachers and left it at that. You have two other oddities with magic. First of all is your apparent lack of any affinities. It's extremely rare for someone to lack any affinities. Not unknown, but very, very rare. It's not especially good or bad- on the one hand, someone without affinities could attune to any type of mana they chose, unlike most mages... but on the other hand, it would be immensely more difficult than normal."

Talia snorted. "Getting to pick your attunement sounds like a blessing to me, so long as you're not afraid of a little work."

Alustin ignored her.

"Then there's Hugh's unusual skill with wards."

Hugh just stared at him. Unusual skill with wards? They were nearly the only spells he could do right, and they clearly weren't that effective, considering how easily Rhodes had gotten through. Also...

"How do you know about my wards, sir?"

Alustin gave him a wry look. "I investigated all three of you extensively before I chose you. Your wards are better than those of many full mages. Most first year wards can't do more than merely make a loud noise when someone crosses over them. Your wards, on the other hand, actively dissuade them from wanting to cross them in the first place. On top of that, they can differentiate between targets- they don't affect you at all. The wards of

33

other first years just affect everyone."

"Is it just a matter of him being able to push more mana into them?" Sabae asked.

Alustin shook his head. "Hardly. Wards are complex, difficult beasts to wrangle. Just pushing more mana in would collapse them. No, Hugh is doing something much more unusual. He's imbuing them with his own will."

"I'm what?" Hugh said.

"You're actively pushing your willforce into your ward spellforms, allowing you far greater control."

"I…" Hugh said, then went quiet. He really had no idea what that meant.

"Will imbuing can be learned, but there's only one type of mage that has no natural affinities alongside a naturally occurring will imbuing talent."

Hugh could feel the other two apprentices staring at him.

"You, Hugh, are what is known as a warlock."

CHAPTER FOUR
Apprentice

Hugh looked around frantically. "I've never made any deals with demons!" he said. He could feel his heart pounding in his chest. Talia and Sabae were both edging away from him in their chairs, looking like they couldn't decide whether to fight or run.

"No one here thinks you've made any…" Alustin said, then sighed. "You haven't been taught what a warlock is, either, have you?"

Hugh had edged back as far in his chair away from Alustin as he could, terrified. "I'm not a warlock!" he squeaked.

Alustin sighed again. "Calm down, Hugh. No one here thinks you've made a contract with a demon." Noticing the expressions on the faces of the other two, he sighed yet again. "Talia, Sabae, he hasn't made any deals with demons. Everything's fine."

Sabae gave Alustin a suspicious look, but seemed to calm down a bit. Talia, on the other hand, looked like she was about to fight Hugh if he even twitched.

"A warlock is a specific type of mage who develops abilities by forming magical pacts with various powerful entities," Alustin said. "Yes, a few warlocks sign contracts with demons for power, but they're very rare. If I even suspected Hugh had made a deal with one, I'd take drastic measures."

Hugh wasn't particularly comforted by that.

"Warlock contracts can be made with all sorts of beings. Elementals, dragons, spirits… even sufficiently powerful magical items. The only requirements are that the being be magical, powerful, and sentient, or at least capable of developing sentience." Alustin pushed his glasses back up his nose. "The gryphon riders of Tsarnassus? They're technically warlocks who have formed magical bonds with their gryphons. Likewise, the Sacred Swordsmen of Havath are warlocks who have formed magical pacts with their weapons." Alustin frowned after mentioning Havath.

"How the hell can you sign a contract with a sword?" Talia asked.

"The answer is long and involved, so let's leave it for another time," Alustin said. "For now, you just need to know that warlocks get to choose the being they contract with. They should choose very, very carefully- their choice determines the attunements and abilities they get, and if they don't negotiate carefully, the terms can be very, very bad. And I wouldn't go around telling people Hugh's a warlock, either- their bad reputation might not be entirely earned, but that won't matter to a lot of people."

The other two finally seemed to have stopped giving Hugh suspicious looks.

"Of course, Hugh wouldn't be nearly so interesting if he were an ordinary warlock."

Hugh didn't like the sound of that very much.

"Most warlocks have minuscule mana reservoirs. They don't need them- they get power through their contracts. Hugh, however, with his massive mana reservoir, offers some... interesting possibilities."

The three apprentices sat silently for a moment. Alustin watched them, then smiled.

"So! Time to discuss your classes!"

Alustin was having all three of them drop all of their magic related classes- they'd only be taking History and Mathematics normally, and he was transferring them all to morning classes. Afternoons, apparently, were all his- something he said with a rather sinister smile.

Before they left, Alustin handed each of his apprentices a book. Talia received a thin little volume entitled simply "Dreamfire." Sabae received a slightly larger manual of mana channeling techniques- albeit one that looked much older than even Hugh's books of wards. Hugh, however, received a truly massive tome that required both hands to hold. The book was entirely bound in leather- though not, Hugh suspected, from anything as common as a cow- and embossed with intricate spellform diagrams.

"Galvachren's Bestiary?" Hugh said. "Sir, I've read lots of bestiaries. They're all mutually contradictory nonsense."

Alustin smiled. "Most of them have at least a few grains of truth, but yes, they're mostly nonsense. Galvachren, however, produces the finest bestiary on the continent. He's also somehow managed to enchant all of the copies so that he can update them whenever he needs to. When I got my first copy, I was your age, and the book was only half that size."

Hugh stared at the book in astonishment. It would still be the biggest book Hugh had ever read even if it were half its current size. It must weigh at least twenty pounds.

"Why do I need a bestiary, sir?"

"To start researching for potential contracts, of course. You'll want to jump to the section on individual entities powerful enough to deserve their own entries, it's near the back."

It was Hugh's turn to sigh as he lifted the book.

"You can all go for now, though I expect to see you all here tomorrow," Alustin said. "One thing before you leave, however: Please stop calling me Master or Sir. Alustin will be fine."

As they left the office, Hugh immediately strode off back towards his hidden lair, carrying his new book in both hands. He didn't even notice that Sabae looked like she wanted to speak to Talia and him. Hugh took his usual circuitous route through the stacks to get home, dodging origami golems on the way, then sidled behind the bookshelf to get into his lair. It was much, much harder than usual, considering the sheer size of Galvachren's

Bestiary.

When he got inside, he stopped in shock. His room was completely different. His makeshift bed had been replaced by an actual mattress with a bed frame. His rickety furniture had been replaced by much sturdier furniture, and the shelves lined with books on warlocks, grimoires of wards, and even, he noticed, a few novels. There was a clock atop one of the shelves. Glow crystals had even been installed in his walls. Even his window was different- there were curtains now, and the warped frame with the discolored glass had been replaced by a brand new, well-made window.

There was a note lying on his new bed. It read: "I can't be having any student of mine sleeping on a bed of trash." It was signed *Alustin Haber, Librarian Errant.*

Hugh stared at the note in surprise for a while, then dropped the bestiary on his desk to examine his wards. As best as he could tell, the wards were completely untouched. Surprised, he sat down on his bed.

Hugh started trying to figure out how Alustin had gotten through the wards- or, for that matter, gotten an entire bed into his lair- just since he'd last been in the room that morning. It was at that point that the events of the day caught up to him.

Hugh burst into tears.

Phragmos Mast-Biter: *Phragmos is a foul-tempered Kraken off the northern Ithonian coast. He dwells in a massive sea cave underneath one of the cliffs coming off the northern Skyreach mountains. Quite a few fleets and powerful mages have challenged Phragmos, but none have ever returned. He doesn't always attack passing ships, but sailors are well advised to stay far from his cave.*

What kind of powers would forming a pact with a kraken give him? The ability to breathe underwater, maybe? Supernatural strength? A water attunement? And what kind of price would a kraken demand in return?

Asterion: *Asterion is a truly unique creature. He resembles a minotaur in form, if a minotaur were twenty feet tall and made entirely of a piece of the starry night sky hauled to earth, with eyes like suns. Asterion roams up and down the Skyreach Mountains, and is rarely to be found in the same place twice. He's only been seen visiting the same place a few times- an ancient, ruined city that predates the Ithonian Empire. He seldom pays attention to humans and avoids settlements. When irritated, however, he is an implacable foe. Asterion has never been seen to eat or sleep.*

It had taken hours for Hugh to finally relax. He'd worked himself near to hysteria the last few days with worry over the Choosing, but it had gone better than he'd ever truly anticipated. The revelation that he wasn't worthless as a mage had been an even bigger shock yet.

Zzthkxz: *Zzthkxz is an elephant sized spider found in the depths of the Labyrinth below Skyhold. This huge arachnid enjoys asking riddles of and toying with her prey before carrying back to her web to become part of her larder.*

Hugh was a little startled to find mention of a monster below Skyhold. He'd heard of the Labyrinth before, of course- it was mentioned in most of the stories about

Skyhold, and first year students were frequently warned never to enter it. It was filled with traps and roaming monsters, to say nothing of the simple threat of getting lost in its passages. It far predated Skyhold, and was thought by many to be one of the main reasons Skyhold was built where it was- for all its dangers, adventurers and mages willing to brave its depths often returned with powerful magical items and rare magical substances.

Heliothrax: Heliothrax is an ancient sun wyrm, a dragon of immense size and power. She's quite friendly towards mankind, and has been known to aid mankind against various magical beasts. There are tales of her dating back to the early days of the Ithonian Empire.

Heliothrax sounded far more interesting to Hugh than any entry he'd encountered so far. An ancient sun dragon and defender of mankind? What powers would she grant him? Flight? Light and flame attunements? Heliothrax was going straight to the top of his list. A part of Hugh couldn't help but think that forming a pact with Heliothrax would overshadow even apprenticing to Aedan Dragonslayer.

Jaskolskus, the Living Pyroclasm: Jaskolskus is a ash elemental of immense age and power. He seldom leaves the volcanic caldera he resides in, but when stirred to anger is capable of wiping out entire cities.

Hugh wanted to contract with something powerful, but approaching Jaskolskus seemed... well, entirely insane. Elementals were difficult to communicate with or understand at the best of times, not to mention easy to

anger. And an elemental as powerful as Jaskolskus…
Nope.

Karna Scythe: *Karna Scythe is the newest queen of the gorgons, only having held power for about a century and a half. Unlike most gorgon queens of the past, she's proven willing to tolerate human visits to the labyrinth her people guard, and even engage in trade with some humans.*

Dawn was closer than dusk by the time Hugh finally left the bestiary on his desk (open to the entry of Ephyrus, the Fallen Moon, an immense jellyfish that floated through stormclouds above the jungles of southeast Ithos) to go to sleep.

CHAPTER FIVE
Lessons

The next morning, Alustin's apprentices met at his office. Hugh was the last to arrive- living in the library didn't do much to prevent oversleeping after staying up too late.

Talia opened her mouth to say something- a complaint about Hugh being late, he wagered- but before she could say it the door popped open and Alustin poked his head out.

"Excellent, you're all here! Come in!"

Hugh hurried in after Alustin to avoid a confrontation with Talia. He headed for the chairs in front of Alustin's desk, only to have Alustin snag him by the shoulder and turn him towards one wall, where one of the chalkboards had been erased.

"Second lesson!" Alustin said.

"Second lesson?" Hugh said.

"I'm not actually keeping track," Alustin said.

Hugh thought better of responding to that.

Talia and Sabae caught up with them as Alustin began drawing on the chalkboard.

"So you wanted to know about the Aether," Alustin said.

"Not really," Talia said.

"The Aether is like the ocean," Alustin said, rapidly drawing a crude picture of the sea. Hugh noted that it looked nothing like the beautiful drawings on the other walls.

"What's the Aether, and why do we care if it's like the ocean?" Talia said.

Alustin turned to look at them. "The Aether is where mages get all of their power. It is pure mana that permeates every corner of the world. And, like I said, it is like the sea."

"Are there fish?" Talia asked. Hugh was fairly confident she was being sarcastic.

Alustin opened his mouth to answer, but Sabae spoke first. "Will you quit interrupting? You might not have any interest in learning, but we do." Talia glared back at Sabae- and, to his discomfort, Hugh as well. He looked away quickly.

Before Talia could interject again, Alustin spoke up. "I certainly hope there's no fish in the Aether. That's... something of a terrifying thought." He shook his head. "Anyhow, it's like the ocean in that the Aether ebbs and flows like water. It has currents and depths, and prefers to take the path of least resistance. Unlike water, however, it cares not for what lies in its way or the pull of gravity. It flows freely, unless…"

Alustin turned back to the chalkboard and resumed adding details to the seascape. He said nothing for a moment, until Hugh realized that he was waiting on someone to answer.

"Unless it's forced into moving!" Talia said. Sabae glared at her.

"I highly, highly recommend against trying to force the Aether currents to do anything. Have you ever tried forcing the ocean to do anything?" Alustin said, not even turning away from his drawing.

That actually seemed to give Talia pause.

"You can't force the Aether to move, but you may forge channels for it to flow through. Your body does this naturally, absorbing and storing mana from the Aether. Spellforms may then be used to take your stored mana and utilize it. As your body absorbs mana from the Aether, it drains the mana around you. Then, at a speed that depends on the density of the Aether nearby, it fills back up, like a pond filling in the hole left by a bucket."

"Is it possible to channel mana directly from the Aether, instead of letting it refill your mana reservoirs?" Hugh asked.

Alustin hesitated in his drawing. "Hypothetically, but it's so dangerous and of so little benefit that few try it. The mana of the Aether is pure and unattuned, and has few uses. It only becomes attuned within your body. It's better to wait for your body to refill your mana reservoirs naturally. Those that have tried it generally only do so for the sake of saying they have." He looked contemplative for a moment.

"Back to the topic of our lecture. The natural ebb and

flow of the Aether results in huge differences in the available mana. Some places, like Emblin," nodding at Hugh as he mentioned Emblin, "have Aether with such low density that a few paltry cantrips can leave it dry for hours. Other places, like Skyhold, have such rich and dense mana fields that thousands of mages casting spells daily can't even make a noticeable dent. Of course, you can still exhaust yourself casting spells- the Aether around here refills much more quickly than your mana reservoirs will."

Alustin turned back towards them. Somehow, he'd turned the crude drawing into a gorgeously detailed landscape. Hugh had genuinely never thought chalk capable of portraying that level of detail.

"So, what's the next question I want you to ask?" Alustin said.

The apprentices were silent for a moment, and then Sabae spoke up. "Where does the mana come from?"

Alustin smiled. "Exactly."

Talia spoke up. "Everyone knows that one. It comes from life itself."

Alustin's smile vanished, and he wagged his finger. "What did I say about things that everyone knows, Talia?"

He whirled back around to face the chalkboard again and drew a circle. "That was the leading theory for many centuries, but there's one huge, gaping hole in the idea. Namely, that mana deserts and mana rich regions don't seem to correspond to what's living there. The Endless Erg, for instance, is quite desolate, aside from a few monsters, and yet has incredibly rich mana. Emblin, on the other hand, is largely covered in pine forests, and yet has next to no mana. Scholars came up with thousands of explanations for this seeming paradox, each more intricate than the last. Eventually, the whole house of cards came tumbling down around half a century ago. We don't need to go into all the details, but what we now believe to be the source of the Aether?"

By now Alustin had fleshed out the circle into a detailed map of Anastis, with the continent of Ithos front and center. He'd marked Emblin and the Endless Erg on the map as he mentioned them.

"It's the death of the universe itself."

The apprentices were silent at Alustin's proclamation. The first thing that popped in Hugh's head was that Alustin really, really enjoyed dramatic pauses.

"The what of the what now?" Talia said. She looked as startled as Hugh felt. Sabae, of course, hadn't shown a reaction other than narrowing her eyes a little.

"The universe," Alustin continued, apparently pleased at their reactions, "is slowly wearing down over the countless eons. On some far distant day in the future-likely long after the last human has withered to dust and the last star has been extinguished- it will grind to a halt. This slow weathering of the fabric of the universe itself is what generates the Aether- it's a waste product of the dying of the universe."

Hugh took a few moments to process this. He opened his mouth to ask another question, but Alustin seems to have already moved on. "We're off to the library. As my apprentices, you'll all be permitted into the uppermost restricted level, but don't attempt to go any deeper- not only is it forbidden, it's dangerous. Magical libraries tend to have a life of their own." Before any of his apprentices could react, he was already striding towards the door.

As they followed him out of the office, he once more whirled to walk backwards facing them. "So, Sabae: Tell me what you thought of that book of mana channeling techniques."

Sabae sighed. "They're all useless. They require you to channel mana at such high densities that any spells cast with them would be incredibly hard to control even without my... difficulties." She unconsciously rubbed at some of the branching scars on her hands as she said this. "If I tried to cast a spell channeled like that, it'd turn out even worse than usual."

Alustin smiled. "That was, in fact, exactly why those techniques haven't seen use in centuries. There was a brief fashion of casting overpowered, uncontrolled spells in the decades after the fall of the Ithonian Empire- it was supposed to display your primal nature, or some such ridiculousness. I'm going to need you to start practicing those techniques immediately."

Sabae actually showed emotion at this. She started to splutter, but Alustin had already addressed Hugh as he led them down a staircase- still walking backwards- into a section of the library that first year students weren't allowed into. This was the first section to contain more advanced grimoires, as well as some actually enchanted books.

"So, has our resident warlock chosen any potential contractees?" Hugh had, in fact, brought a long list of potentials, starting with Heliothrax. "Warlocks have tried to contract with Heliothrax for centuries, she has no interest. A small number of warlocks have made pacts with Asterion, but you have to find him first, which is an immense challenge of its own. Darsammeth would potentially work, but he's one of the most popular entities to sign pacts with- anyone familiar with warlocks would be prepared to face one of his contractors. Ephyrus… bold choice, but we've already got a storm mage," he said, waving at Sabae. In the end, Alustin left only Asterion as an acceptable option. "You're on the right track, though. Keep looking."

Hugh started to ask what, exactly, the right track was, but Alustin had once again moved on. "Talia, how did you enjoy your read last night?"

Talia glared at Alustin. "It was a children's story. A children's story about a mage that made children sleep better by burning away their nightmares with a flame that only existed inside their dreams."

"I admit, it's not the most rigorous scholarly work ever, but it's a start, isn't it?"

Talia glared even harder. "A start to what, helping little children sleep well?"

Alustin laughed at this. "No, to being a battle mage. You'd be wasted as anything else."

"How is a children's tale supposed to help me…"

Alustin, however, had swiveled around to walk forwards again, dodging an origami messenger crane flapping through the air. Hugh was now absolutely convinced that Alustin lived for being dramatic.

"This, my apprentices, is the Great Index."

So far as Hugh could tell, the Great Index was just a dictionary sized volume lying open on a pedestal at the end of a row of shelves. Its pages were blank, and there was a quill pen and an inkwell lying next to it.

Talia pointed down the rows. "That looks like another Great Index fifty feet that way, Al."

Alustin winced. "While I prefer that you not address me as master, I'll have to decline being called Al. And I might have exaggerated a little bit. This book is merely an access node to the Great Index. The Great Index is a semisentient magical construct with the ability to keep track of every volume in this library. At least, every registered volume- there are more than a few that have slipped through the cracks. You can use the Index to search for volumes by their title, subject matter, or even their contents. So let's give it a try, shall we?"

"Crazy librarians?" Talia suggested.

"Dreamfire it is! Excellent suggestion, Talia," Alustin said.

He dipped the pen in the inkwell, then wrote "Dreamfire" on the top of the page. Nothing happened for a few moments, then, in a neat, easily read script, the titles and locations of books began to appear. Alustin waited for it to stop, then with a wink to his apprentices, tore the page out of the book.

Hugh was convinced that another librarian must have heard, and that they were all about to get in trouble, but Alustin merely wrote on two more pages- "Dream attunements" and "Dream manifestations."

He dragged them across the library hunting the titles on the list. As he led them, he began to tell them of dreamfire.

"While it is an amusing tale, that book on dreamfire I had you read was far from a useful one for your needs, Talia. Dreamfire itself is a much, much stranger phenomena. This has to do with the unusual nature of dream attunements, which are among the most versatile attunements out there. They can first be used to alter and manipulate the dreams of a sleeping person. As in the story-book, the most common form of dreamfire is one such technique that can be used to do so." Alustin examined a title on dreamfire for a moment, then reshelved it. "Meddling with the dreams of others, unfortunately, likely won't be possible for you, except for the dreamfire technique. Your tattoos prevent you from channeling dream mana to actually affect the dreams of others otherwise- unless, of course, you wish to make your target dream of fire. So yes, I suppose, I will be training you to purge nightmares from children."

"The second use of dream attunements," Alustin said, handing a title to Talia, "is for illusion. It's much harder to craft illusions with dream attunements than light attunements, but it is quite possible. Sabae, why are you not practicing those mana channeling techniques?"

Sabae jumped. She, like Hugh, had gotten quite absorbed in Alustin's lecture. She mumbled an apology, then her eyes seemed to unfocus as she began concentrating on channeling her mana properly.

"Dream illusions often seem... less solid than light based illusions, but they're far, far more powerful- they can actually hold an element of solidity to them." He handed Talia another book and a scroll. "Which leads to the third use of dream mana- manifesting fragments of dreams physically into the world. It's a powerful, dangerous technique, and one only usable by the most powerful and focused dream mages. Normally it would be at least a decade before you could even attempt it."

"So why are you having me attempt it now?" Talia said.

"Your tattoos, of course," Alustin said, handing her yet another book.

"Shouldn't they make it harder for me to, uh, summon dreams?" Talia said.

"Manifest dreams. And yes, yes they will. With a

49

single exception." He smiled broadly. "Fire."

Talia stared at him wide-eyed for a moment, then smiled broadly. "You're finally talking my language, Al."

Alustin sighed. "Alustin, please. I should note that manifest dreamfire is going to behave very, very differently than normal fire, and I have no idea how your tattoos will alter that, other than significantly. So no experimenting and trying to manifest dreamfire unsupervised, if you please." He added a couple more books to Talia's now huge stack.

"That should about do it for now. Don't forget, however, that dream is only one of your attunements." Alustin glanced at the three pages he'd torn out of the Index, then threw them behind him. Before they hit the ground, however, they folded themselves into origami golems- a dragonfly, a crow, and a winged serpent- and zoomed right back in the direction of the Index access node they came from. Alustin saw Hugh watching them. "The pages will reattach themselves to the access node when you're done with them. It's part of the Index's enchantment."

Alustin led the three of them to another Index access node, where he proceeded to write a series of search terms across pages. Hugh caught "basic spellform theory", "spellform architecture", "formless casting", "warlock contracts", and "mana layering", among others.

"For Hugh," Alustin said, "we're going to be grabbing two types of books. The first type," handing a book to Hugh, "are merely various theoretical guides to warlock contracts. Essential, but a bit bland. I will not, of course, be teaching you to craft an actual warlock contract anytime soon. More excitingly, Hugh, you're going to be reading a number of books on the basic theory behind spellform construction."

This didn't sound particularly exciting to Hugh.

"Unfortunately, I doubt you'll be able to simply start putting less mana into most of your spells, Hugh. You spent the earliest, most critical part of your magical development having to pump entirely too much mana into every effect, even if they were purely subconscious. So we'll need to instead give you different spellforms that can handle the larger mana flow."

That did sound a bit more exciting to Hugh.

"I could give you a simple list of spells to memorize, but that would, in the end, leave you a much, much less flexible mage. Rather like most of the other mages Skyhold produces these days, honestly."

"I'd be happy just being normal, sir." Fantasies about making a pact with a legendary dragon aside, not standing out of the crowd sounded pretty nice to Hugh.

"Alustin, please, not sir," Alustin said, dropping a weighty tome into Hugh's arms, "and merely being normal is hardly something to be happy about. Instead, we're going to make sure that you can improvise spellforms on the fly, so you can have a spell for any occasion."

By the time Alustin was done picking out books for Hugh, he felt like he was going to topple over from the weight of the stack. He glanced over at Talia, who appeared to be trying very, very hard to pretend that the weight of her equally large stack of books wasn't bothering her.

Alustin threw away several more Index pages, which folded themselves up and flew away. "I haven't forgotten you, Sabae. For you, we'll be gathering up more practical manuals on two topics- formless casting and mana layering."

Neither term meant anything to Hugh, but a look of shock came onto Sabae's face. "Formless casting is supposed to be incredibly dangerous! Students are strictly forbidden from attempting it until at least their fourth year."

Alustin chuckled. "Unless your master declares otherwise, that is. Do you know why formless casting is forbidden?"

Sabae started to open her mouth, then hesitated.

"What's this formless casting nonsense?" Talia said.

"Formless casting," Alustin said, "is the practice of casting spells without a spellform. It's faster, more powerful, and has a nasty tendency to result in spells that go horribly, horribly wrong, especially once they've gone more than a few feet away from the caster. Sound familiar?"

Sabae gave him a flat look. "So you're telling me that we're going to solve my inability to cast spells at a distance by learning a way of casting spells that makes it even harder to cast spells at a distance?"

Alustin smiled. "Nope. We're not going to have you cast spells at a distance at all."

Sabae looked like she was about to explode at him when he raised his hand in a placating gesture. "Unfortunately, thanks to your..." Alustin paused, "personal story which you don't want shared, there likely isn't much hope of you ever learning to use spells at any significant range. We are, instead, going to teach you to become an effective close quarters combat mage."

Sabae raised her hands up in the air, showing off her thin, branching scars. "I've tried that, sir. Lightning was never meant to be a close quarters magic."

Alustin smiled. "You've never tried it under my

instruction."

Sabae started to look hopeful for a moment, then her face sank. "Even if you can teach me how to do it, close quarters magic just doesn't work, sir. By the time I close the distance between me and my foe, they'll have had plenty of time to pelt me with spells from afar. That's the reason there aren't any close quarters combat mages."

"Alustin, please, not sir," Alustin said with a sigh. "And as for there not being any close quarters combat mages, I believe Artur Wallbreaker would be surprised to hear it."

Sabae started to say something, then closed her mouth, looking pensive.

"Artur Wallbreaker," Alustin said "has dual iron and stone attunements. He channels them together to create a nigh-unbreakable suit of armor around him during battle, as well as massively empowering that over-sized enchanted hammer he carries everywhere. While he can use his attunements at a distance, he very, very rarely does so, as it drastically reduces the effectiveness of his armor and his hammer. To use his mana the way he does, he uses the second technique I'll be having you read about- mana layering."

Alustin handed Sabae a couple more books. He also spotted a book on the shelf that apparently interested him, and tucked it into his pocket. "Mana layering involves making your mana revolve in extremely tight flows all around your body. It reduces your ability to cast spells at a distance while you're doing it, but that's not a concern with you. It will, eventually, allow you to construct your own magical armor, like Artur does. It'll also likely make several powerful movement techniques available to you, allowing you to close the distance to your foes faster."

Alustin considered another book, started to hand it to Sabae, then changed his mind and reshelved it. "And, by the way, those high density mana channeling exercises I was having you read about? Those will massively enhance the effectiveness of both your mana layering and your formless casting."

Alustin threw aside the last few index pages, which promptly folded themselves into a tiny flock of geese and flew away. "Oh, and Artur Wallbreaker's third secret? Lots and lots of physical and combat training. You'll all, by the way, be learning that."

Hugh was pretty sure that the amount of books they were each carrying already counted as physical training.

CHAPTER SIX

Silence in the Library

Alustin escorted them over to a nearby table, where he simply told them to get reading, and that he'd be back in a few hours.

Hugh couldn't set down his pile of books fast enough. He spent a few moments rubbing his sore muscles before he opened any of the books.

Even though he wanted to dive right into the books on warlock contracts, he made himself pick up one of the books on basic spellform construction instead.

The three had sat there reading silently for around an hour when Sabae slammed her book shut. "So is this how things are going to be for the next few years?" she said, giving them each a flat look. "We're just going to silently pretend the others don't exist?"

"That might be nice," said Talia, glaring at Sabae.

Hugh tucked another book inside the one he was reading as a book mark, then glanced up at the two of them briefly before turning his gaze back to the table.

"We're stuck with each other, so we might as well make the best of the situation," Sabae said.

Talia glared at her for a moment, then sighed. "Fine. What did you have in mind?" She didn't sound especially curious.

Sabae paused for a moment. "Well… why don't we tell each other about ourselves?"

Talia snorted. "You've made it pretty clear that you don't want to tell us about your story already." She glanced at Hugh. "You want to tell us your story, sheepherder?"

Hugh's cheeks heated up. "Not a sheepherder," he said, then opened his book back up.

No one spoke for a few minutes. Hugh noticed, however, that none of them seemed to be turning any pages in their books.

Finally, Sabae spoke again. "My fourth affinity is in healing."

Hugh and Talia looked up in surprise.

"What?" Talia said.

"My fourth affinity is healing," Sabae said.

No one said anything for a moment, then Talia spoke up. "Why would you not want people to find out that you had a healing affinity? They're damn useful."

Hugh didn't have the slightest clue why she wouldn't want people to know, either. Emblin was the only place he'd ever heard of that distrusted healers, and they distrusted all magic.

Sabae hesitated before speaking. "My family has defended the port city of Ras Andis for centuries. Each generation has produced powerful storm mages to shelter the city from storm or invasion. My mother, Andia Kaen Das, is powerful even by the standards of our family. Our family arranged my mother's marriage when she was very young, to the heir of a family of powerful sea mages. They expected her to go along with it quietly, but…" she gave a wry smile, "my mother might be the single most headstrong woman alive."

"Instead of marrying the sea mage, she eloped with my father, a simple healer. My family refused to recognize the relationship for years, and exiled my mother from their estate after she bore me. Even so, they were good years. My father was a kind man, and our family was happy. He ran a small clinic in the city that we lived above. He let people pay what they could, when they could, and earned us many friends among the poor. My mother, rather than compete with the storm mages of her family for work, instead worked as a mere water mage, purifying and tending to wells that were otherwise ignored by the city. The neighborhood councils couldn't pay her much, but they spared what they could. We weren't well off, but we never went wanting."

Sabae paused again. "Then the Blue Death arrived in Ras Andis. A freighter sailed into the city with its crew already sick, but the city failed to quarantine it in time. Within weeks, it had spread through the entire city-especially the poorer neighborhoods."

"What's the Blue Death?" Talia asked.

Sabae was silent for a moment. "Vomiting. High fever. Aches. Then the body temperature begins to plummet. They die almost like they'd walked out into a blizzard, even in the middle of the summer in one of the southernmost cities of Ithos."

Sabae idly played with one of her books. "My father died tending to the poor. He might have staved off the disease himself, but for how much energy he expended healing others. Many in my family died as well, and they finally reached out to my mother once more. For a time my mother resisted, thinking that they only wanted her back because my father had died, but something had broken in her with my father's death. We were welcomed back with open arms. I was eight."

"Those years were not bad ones. My family was kind and considerate of me, a bastard child they'd hardly met before. They treated me as though I'd always been there. I often felt out of place and uncomfortable with our family's wealth, but they were always patient and kind. I think that they truly regretted their rejection of my mother over the years, and had wanted to take her back long before, but could not bring themselves to until the tragedy of the plague.

"My mother, however, began to chafe at living at the family estates. She soon began accepting shipboard contracts, shepherding merchant fleets safely through stormy waters. She rarely came home, and seldom for more than a couple of weeks."

"A few years later, my affinities manifested. My family was excited at first- they had expected me to have perhaps one or two of the family affinities, likely alongside healing. Children rarely inherit all of their parents' affinities. Instead, I had all three and healing. Then, of course, my curse manifested instead. They genuinely tried to teach me to control my magic farther than a few inches from my body, but all attempts failed in the end. Even my mother, on one of her rare visits back, proved unable to help."

"They never blamed me, and never treated me badly, but I could tell that they all considered it the fault of my parents, that they blamed my father for polluting the Kaen Das line. What made it worse is that they were right. Many healers, like my father, completely lack the ability to do magic at a distance, in exchange for greater control up close. They seldom feel the lack, but it ruined me as a storm mage."

"My family sent me to Skyhold in hopes of a solution, and the school readily offered their help- no school had ever had the patronage of our clan before, and I hope you understand that I do not mean to be arrogant when I say that it is of considerable worth. I am the first Kaen Das ever sent for schooling in the magical arts outside of our family, and likely the last as well. Not, in truth, that I am much of a Kaen Das. Since I arrived, however, the teachers, unable to come up with a simple solution, have distanced themselves from me, not wanting my failure associated with them. Some students have tried to befriend me, but only for my family's reputation and wealth. A few teachers have tried to teach me healing, but healing is what ruined me as a storm mage, and I will not deepen my family's shame by learning it."

There was silence for a moment. Then Talia finally spoke up. "I bet it's going to feel good rubbing your powers in their face in a few years." She grinned at Sabae. Sabae blinked for a moment, then a faint smile crossed her face as well. Hugh grinned a little himself, but ducked his head when the other two looked at him.

"I'd never let myself hope before I met Alustin," Sabae said. "If he can teach us what he promised…"

"Unless he's just completely insane," Talia said, smiling.

Hugh somehow found the nerve to crack a joke. "Can't it be both?"

Talia snorted with amusement, and Sabae chuckled quietly. Hugh found himself smiling a little.

They were all silent for a moment until Talia spoke up. "I suppose it's my turn to tell a story."

"Clan Castis," said Talia, "is not the biggest of the clans of the Northern Skyreach Mountains. In fact, it's one of the smallest. It isn't the richest, nor the oldest, nor the best positioned. It is, however, one of the most feared. We've stood a thousand battles and won a thousand battles." She grinned. "Well, most of a thousand battles."

Hugh doubted this was much of an exaggeration. The northern mountain clans were famous for their belligerence and territorial behavior. They constantly raided each other and many neighboring countries, most of which eventually just decided it was cheaper to pay them tribute each year than to try and root them out. Not that it wasn't tried repeatedly, but even the Ithonian Empire had never fully conquered the clans.

"The secret to our success is twofold. The first is our command of fire. Over half the tribe are fire mages. Many of them are quite weak, but quite a few each generation are extremely powerful. In large numbers, though, even the weak fire mages are a force to be reckoned with. We're not versatile in our magic, but with fire, you don't have to be."

"In each generation, one of the most powerful fire mages is chosen as warleader. Not necessarily the most

59

powerful fire mage is chosen- the elders also judge candidates by their wisdom, courage, and other qualities. The warleader only leads the tribe in battle, but we have a great many battles." She smiled at that.

"My father, like his mother before him and her father before that, was chosen as warleader. He was the second most powerful fire mage in his generation."

"My mother was his chiefest rival for warleader in his generation. She was even more powerful than my father. In the end, what cost her the position was two things- her tiny stature and her unquenchable temper." She smiled to herself. "She hated my father for years after that. Only after he'd proven himself in battle time and time again did she allow him to court her."

"I am the youngest of seven children. Each and every one of my brothers is a powerful fire mage. Several of them are, in fact, even more powerful than either of our parents. Our territory has already expanded greatly since they began joining our battles. One will assuredly be the next warleader. And then I was born."

"My parents had long wanted a daughter. My parents would gladly have spoiled me, but I never had the patience for ribbons or toys. I was wandering into the mountains and fighting other children from the day I could walk." She looked particularly proud of that fact. "My parents, expecting me to be a fire mage as powerful as any of my brothers, went to the elders of my tribe early for my tattoos."

She pulled back her sleeves, revealing more of her tattoos. They were clearly spellforms, but of incredible complexity. "These tattoos are the second half of our success. My tribe has spent countless generations experimenting and learning. We tried countless patterns, inks, and other variables. We sought out enchanters, other fire mages, other clans that enchanted tattoos. Several generations ago, one of my mother's ancestors even traveled to another continent to learn from a tribe there who used tattoos to improve their mastery over wind."

"Our tattoos increase our attunement to fire to an unparalleled degree, beyond even our techniques and training passed down through countless generations. They also make us highly resistant to heat and fire. We are the mightiest fire mages on the planet. Even our non-mages are tattooed with different spellforms that provide fire resistance beyond that of our mages."

"Why...?" Sabae began.

Talia lowered her hands and shook her head. "Too much of the fire resistance spellforms can begin to interfere with a mages offensive power."

Talia grew pensive. "There's a side effect to the tattoos, however. They interfere with other attunements. Not that there are many other attunements present in our tribe, but we do intermarry with other tribes. Normally, that's not a problem. You can't use the other attunements, but you can still use fire."

"My parents, however, had me tattooed even before my gifts began to manifest. The earlier you can catch the gifts manifesting, the deeper the attunement to flame can be. Tattooing before one's gifts even begin manifesting results in the deepest attunement of all, but it's a risk seldom taken, for if one isn't a mage, their tattoos are a waste, and their fire resistance cannot further be improved. With six brothers and two parents who all number among our tribe's greatest mages, however? No one thought it was a risk. If that weren't enough, my parents had the elders design me the most elaborate, powerful tattoos our tribe had ever attempted up to that point- a design that wouldn't even work unless it was tattooed before one's gifts begin to manifest."

Talia's frown grew deeper. "And then my gifts did manifest. Bone and dream. My gifts were useless, and my father was furious. He thought my mother must have slept with a man of a different tribe. They burnt down several acres of alpine forest in their arguing. Eventually, seers confirmed I was truly his daughter, but…" she grinned briefly, "my mother made him sleep with the dogs and goats for weeks before she let him come back inside. Clan Castis rode out on raids many times during those weeks."

"My parents and the elders of my tribe journeyed far and wide for answers. My brothers each traveled to a different nation, to consult their wisest sages. Each failed, one by one, until only my eldest brother had not returned. On Midwinter, months after he had left, he returned to Clan Castis with word from Skyhold that they would take me. They made no promises, but they offered hope. Clan Castis has never sent its children to learn from the great academies before. We would bind ourselves to no nation, but Skyhold, of all the great schools of magic, has no allegiance to any nation."

Talia frowned. "Upon arriving here, though, I found myself ignored and dismissed by teachers and students alike as a useless barbarian. Many even thought of me as illiterate, even when I showed them I could read." Talia gave the other two a brief challenging look. "After all, there is little else to do but read and tell stories when winter traps us in our cabins and lodges."

"It seems that the faculty here thought my brother had exaggerated, that my problems were easily solved by anyone not a foolish barbarian. When it proved otherwise, they turned away rather than face their own shortcomings. Alustin is the first one to offer anything but dismissal in months. Truly, I had planned to simply walk away from Skyhold before Alustin chose me."

They were all silent for a moment, then the girls turned to face Hugh. He realized that they intended him to tell his story. He felt his cheeks start to grow red, and looked back and forth between the two.

Sabae seemed to take pity on him. "Take your time, Hugh. We're not going to bite you." She gave a pointed glance at Talia, who didn't notice.

Talia, who had been staring intently at Hugh, spoke up. "I… need to apologize to you, Hugh. I've been acting an ass towards you- both of you, really. You haven't done anything to deserve it." She said this, of course, with a fierce glare, as if daring either of them to reject her apology.

"Don't worry about it," Sabae said. "Your story makes your anger entirely understandable."

Hugh, in a quiet voice, simply said "Thank you." He looked Talia directly in the eyes as he did so, though he looked away immediately afterwards.

Talia seemed to relax a bit. Hugh, on the other hand, tensed up as the other two looked back at him and he realized that they actually wanted to hear his story.

Talia and Sabae's stories were like something out of a story. They had the kind of pasts that heroes out of tales did. Hugh… Hugh had the story of a nobody. No-one could possibly… Hugh stopped that line of thinking and a few deep, calming breaths. Then a few more. Then one last, long breath.

"I… I don't have any mages in my family. No grand

history, no prized family name. We were just simple village folk. We lived in Cedarvale, a little village high up in the alpine forests of Emblin. My father ran Cedarvale's lumber mill, my mother was a lumber merchant's daughter. Simple folk. Not wealthy, except by the standards of Cedarvale." He looked up and grinned nervously. "There were only about four hundred people living in and around Cedarvale, so the standards weren't particularly impressive."

Hugh stopped talking for a few moments. He stared at the table, trying to sort through his thoughts. Out of the corner of his eye, he say Talia open her mouth to say something, but Sabae shook her head.

"When I was ten, our house burned down. My father carried me out, but when he went back for my mother and baby sister, the roof collapsed."

He went silent for a few more moments.

"My father's brother and his wife took me in. They were sheepherders, and had eight children already. My uncle sold my father's mill, so they should have been able to afford to care for me easily, but always complained of the cost and the difficulty."

Hugh 's voice took a bitter turn. "They hardly spent anything on me. They dressed me in hand-me-downs from my cousins and made sure they were all fed first. They put me to work with the sheep, and I was willing- but they never bothered to teach me anything or help me, and I've always been small for my age. They soon made it very, very clear I was useless as a sheepherder. Whenever my cousins and I argued, my aunt and uncle would never take my side. We lived far out of town, so there weren't other children to play with. I ended up spending most days out wandering the woods."

"They never meant to be cruel or neglectful. They were just too busy to spare much thought to me. Having me out of their hair most of the time was a blessing. The instant my powers started manifesting, they shipped me right off to Skyhold. Emblin is suspicious of magic, and prides themselves of their lack of mages. My aunt and uncle made it clear I wasn't welcome back, and they haven't written since."

"Since I got here… it's… I…". He took a deep breath. "No one wants to be friends with a country bumpkin who can't do the smallest piece of magic right. The only thing I'm good for is as the butt of jokes. A few teachers tried to help me, but until Alustin came along they all gave me up as a waste of time."

Hugh felt out of breath- it'd been quite literally years since he'd talked so much. He hadn't looked up once since he started the story- he was sure the other two would be scornful of how… bucolic and back-woodsy his story was.

As the silence stretched on, he felt his face start to heat up and turn red, but he didn't look up. Finally, Talia spoke up. "Hugh."

Despite himself, Hugh looked up. Sabae looked sympathetic, but Talia looked absolutely furious. He felt his cheeks grow even redder, and he wanted to sink into his chair.

"Your family isn't worth the water they drink. Anyone who would treat their own blood like that in need are honorless snakes, and they deserve to get sheared with their own sheep. Though I reckon it's probably hard to tell the difference."

Hugh just stared at her, mouth open. Then he looked at Sabae, whose expression looked slightly startled. Sabae's expression quickly grew resolute, however, and she nodded at him. Hugh looked back and forth for a few more moments.

Then he burst out laughing. It really wasn't that funny, but he'd been so wound up and stressed while telling his story that he couldn't help it. Any reaction other than scorn was completely unexpected, and actually getting angry for him?

The other two stared at him for a few seconds as he just kept laughing. He tried to stop laughing to explain, then started laughing even harder. After a few more seconds, Sabae's normally reserved facade broke fully, and she started chuckling as well.

Talia glared furiously at both of them. This just made Hugh and Sabae laugh even harder. She looked like she was about to start yelling at them, but when she opened her mouth a laugh popped out as well.

When Alustin arrived a few moments later, he found all of them laughing hysterically. Talia had actually fallen on the floor. It might have been the first time they'd ever seen Alustin look surprised.

That just made them laugh even harder.

CHAPTER SEVEN

Training

Hugh's life began settling into a routine after that. He started each day very, very early with a quick breakfast. After that, it was time to exercise. Alustin hadn't even remotely been joking about the physical training. He had them doing strength training exercises and running laps around one of the larger training rooms. What made it even worse is that Alustin would run alongside them, actually giving them lectures as he did so- on the nature of the Aether, on common attunements, on their own attunements, on the utility of cantrips (and their sore under-use by most mages), and countless other topics. He'd expect them to listen, and to answer questions, even while completely out of breath.

Then it was time to clean up for their history and mathematics classes. Hugh normally didn't have any trouble with math- he'd always been decent, if not great, at it. Being exhausted every day he had it, however, didn't help him much. He fell asleep more than a few times in both classes. Where before he would have remained asleep until the teacher noticed, Sabae or Talia would wake him up now- Sabae generally a bit gentler than Talia. When he needed to, he returned the favor.

After that, it was time for lunch. They were usually too tired to talk much, but Hugh still valued the time with others. Hugh wasn't sure the other two counted him as a friend, but they didn't seem to dislike his company.

Their magical training each day began after that. Hugh was drilled on the basic construction principles of spellforms until he began seeing their geometric shapes in his dreams. He wasn't learning any actual spells yet, unfortunately. Even with Alustin's promises, it didn't feel like he'd improved that much as a mage.

Except, of course, when it came to wards. Alustin had thrown book after book of ward design and theory at him, giving him lecture after lecture. The book throwing wasn't always metaphorical, either- once Hugh had begun crafting wards meant to guard him against physical attacks, Alustin started throwing books, pens, and any other objects he had to hand at Hugh.

He also demanded that Hugh grow faster and faster at crafting the wards, often giving Hugh just a few moments to prepare a basic ward circle before beginning to throw things. Hugh began carrying several sticks of chalk with him in the pockets of his trousers so that he could always be ready to craft a ward.

Hugh also continued to work his way through the immense bestiary. Incredibly few of the entities he chose met with Alustin's approval. Thus far, his list was still only three entries long- Asterion, the starry minotaur spirit, Uolos, an immense frost serpent dwelling in the far north, and Dagan Spireborn, the ghost of a warrior who died centuries ago keeping a narrow mountain pass clear of monsters, and who still maintained his vigil.

Alustin hadn't given Hugh a lot of clues about his upcoming plans, but he had let slip that he intended to take the three of them out of Skyhold next summer in order to gain Hugh a contract, as well as to test the abilities of all three of the apprentices.

Sabae and Talia had personalized training programs of their own, as well as being taught more cantrips- Alustin was obsessed with cantrips, apparently. Sabae spent hours every day practicing her high density mana channeling and mana layering. When she got to the point where she could carry out either one effectively, Alustin started her on practicing both at once. Hugh got used to seeing breezes blow in a narrow circle around her, and to the occasional loud bang as her mana got loose from her control. The tall girl hadn't been started on formless casting yet, but Alustin had her learning the theory and doing mental exercises to prepare her for it.

She also spent an hour each day doing physical combat training, separately from Talia and Hugh. She spent many of those days with Artur Wallbreaker, who was apparently pleased to have a regular sparring partner for his son. Sabae also met regularly with a succession of guards, traveling adventurers passing through to delve into the Labyrinth, and other warriors to teach her various lessons. She focused primarily upon unarmed combat techniques, but was introduced to a great many weapons and weapon styles, so that she could be familiar with them in case she came up against them.

Alustin had tried to convince Sabae a number of times that she should start developing her healing affinity into a full attunement, but had been entirely unsuccessful. Sabae had absolutely no interest in doing so. Even now that she was being taught battle magic, she still seemed to blame her healing gift for her inability to follow her family's traditions and training.

Talia's training consisted of hours and hours sitting unmoving, trying to manifest dreamfire. Hugh hadn't realized how rare dream attunements were and how difficult to control they were, even without Talia's disadvantages. There were, apparently, few enough dream attuned at Skyhold that they could be counted on the fingers of one hand. Many with dream affinities were actively discouraged from pursuing attunement with them if they had any other affinities to focus on. Of those that did pursue dream attunement, many died during training. Manifest dreams were as chaotic and protean as actual dreams, and a manifested dream sword could easily transform into a serpent and bite its wielder. It took singular force of will to control the form of manifest dreams.

She had only managed it a handful of times so far. Once the candle-flame of dreamfire she'd successfully manifested transformed into a cloud of stinging bugs that vanished after leaving welts on the three of them. (Alustin, of course, was untouched.) A second time the flames had frozen solid, fallen to the floor, and shattered into nothing. The few times she managed to manifest stable dreamfire, it had an unearthly appearance- it burned an unstable purple-green color, and the light it cast made objects seem to warp and twist.

Her work with dream-based illusions was progressing a little more swiftly, but not in a particularly useful way. Her illusions only showed up in the shape of flames, albeit flames made of horses, trees, castles, dragons, and other fragmentary dream shapes. Talia would never make for much of an illusionist.

Unfortunately, Alustin hadn't yet figured out a way for her to use her bone attunement. He claimed he had a couple of promising leads, but nothing more. Dream's versatility was easier to use with Talia's spellform tattoos than the relatively more focused nature of bone attunements.

At the end of the day, Hugh would head off to eat dinner by himself in the smaller dining hall. He usually spent a little bit of time reading his assigned texts and browsing the Bestiary once he got back to his hidden lair, but as often as not he just passed out in bed the instant he got back.

Kleteletet, the Cloud Serpent: *Kleteletet is a forty foot long serpent made entirely of venomous mists made solid. It only appears on moonless nights in the jungles of southeast Ithos, and its victims take hours to die inside its stomach, unable to escape, although their screams make it out just fine.*

Hugh definitely wasn't adding Kleteletet to his list.

Every Fifthday, the students were all given the day off. With the grueling training schedule Alustin ran them through, Hugh needed it- and assumed the others did too. Hugh generally stayed in his secret room in the stacks reading. He was still looking for a entity to contract with.

Tetragnath: *Tetragnath is a hive mind spanning millions of spiders. Their webs completely cover huge portions of the Aito forest in Tsarnassus. In the depths of Tetragnath's web are supposedly found a number of incredibly rare plants in high demand by alchemists. Few make it out alive from its forest, but burning down the woods to clear out Tetragnath would also burn the valued plants, and Tetragnath shows little interest in expanding its territory, so it's tolerated more than most similar threats.*

There were a surprising number of spiders listed in Galvachren's Bestiary. Apparently magical spiders became intelligent and powerful enough to be listed in it quite often. Or, possibly, Hugh just kept reading the sections with more spiders in them. It was hard to tell, given how often the book changed. Galvachren apparently added entries to the book on almost a daily basis, as well as regularly moving entries around within it. There didn't seem to be any sense to the orders of the entries, either.

Chelys Mot, the Earthshaker: Chelys Mot is a turtle of immense size, with a shell almost a hundred feet across. He has the ability to control earth and stone, and is even capable of generating localized earthquakes. He is short-tempered and dislikes being disturbed, but can be reasoned or bargained with if one is polite. He generally moves around on the northern edge of the Endless Erg.

Hugh whistled. Chelys Mot seemed like an excellent option. Powerful, approachable, and relatively close by. He quickly wrote him down on the list of entities to show Alustin.

Intet Slew, the Blood Boiler: This half dragon, half demon creature has a habit of...

Hugh paled a bit. Nope. Definitely not Intet Slew. Not a chance.

Lasnabourne, the Seaflame: Lasnabourne is an ancient phoenix who nests atop one of the volcanic jungle islands to the southwest of the Ithonian continent. This phoenix isn't hostile towards humans, often engaging in conversations to hear the news from the continent. He eats mostly whales and sharks caught in the sea nearby. Interestingly, unlike other phoenixes, his flames don't seem to be dimmed at all by water, and he can sometimes be seen deep below the surface, still burning brightly as he dives for his prey.

Hugh added Lasnabourne to the list. Talia would be interested in hearing about Lasnabourne's underwater flames, as well.

It'd been about three weeks since the Choosing, and Hugh was happier than he'd been in years. Aedan was apparently a demanding master, as Rhodes hadn't had the time to harass him at all during that time. The privacy his secret library room afforded him was genuinely soothing- especially now that he'd been able to apply his progressively improving skill at wards to his room. And even if Talia and Sabae didn't consider him a friend, they were at least friendly towards him.

Keayda, the Merchant of Truths: *This ancient naga lich's library is one of the greatest in the world, and to any who bring Keayda knowledge, books, or scrolls he doesn't yet possess, he is willing to grant answers of equivalent value. Keayda is known to have an especial interest in historical texts. Those who cross Keayda or try to steal from him, however, get their skin turned into parchment for his journals.*

Huh. What sorts of affinities would a naga lich bequeath on him? Naga, beings with the torsos of humans, but with long snake tails instead of legs, could have as many different affinities as humans, though poison affinities were far more common among them than among humans. Since he was a lich, a form of sentient undead, maybe he'd grant Hugh a bone affinity? The turning skin to parchment thing was a bit ominous, but Hugh didn't have any intention of stealing from Keayda. He thought for a moment, then wrote Keayda's name on the list.

Andas Thune: *This relatively young dragon has already carved out a surprisingly large territory for himself from those of his older, larger draconic neighbors. This lightning dragon is also an incredibly capable illusionist, and...*

Hugh's stomach rumbled. It was about time for lunch, so he dragged himself away from his desk and put his shoes on. Before he left, he opened his window to look out. Even this early in the spring, the days were brutally hot. Skyhold stayed a fairly consistent temperature year round, thanks partially to powerful enchantments, but mostly because it was largely underground.

Hugh watched a sandship pull into Skyhold's port. A flock of lesser desert drakes, no bigger than geese, playfully weaved in and out of its masts and sails. To either side of him, he could see people bustling around the balconies, walkways, and courtyards of Skyhold. He smiled and turned to go.

Hugh's smile lasted him all the way out the library and well on his way to the dining hall.

Then he heard a voice that made his smile drop away like it had never been there at all.

"Sheepherder!" Rhodes called.

Hugh winced. This was just what he needed. This is

what he got for not paying better attention to his surroundings. He turned around slowly to face Rhodes, who was standing in the middle of the hallway intersection that Hugh had just passed.

Rhodes had a huge smile plastered on his face. "I've missed you, sheepherder! My master has kept me so busy that I'm sure you've forgotten your place by now."

Rhodes was accompanied by the blue haired and eyed twins that Sulassa Tidecaller had picked at the Choosing. Both the boy and the girl were giving Hugh amused looks. Hugh scowled and looked down at the ground, preparing to run.

"Nothing to say to me, sheepherder? That's too bad. I was hoping to hear a little bit about your new master. You know, the librarian."

"I'm not a sheepherder," Hugh muttered.

The twins laughed, and Hugh clenched his fists.

"What's he teaching you? How to shelve books? No, he'd have to teach you to read first. Was he really that desperate that he'd need an illiterate sheepherder for an apprentice?" Rhodes laughed, and the twins laughed along with him.

"Maybe he's teaching you a little paper magic? Now there's an affinity useless enough that you might have a chance with it."

Hugh's fists clenched even tighter. Though in truth, he actually didn't know what Alustin's attunements were- the few times one of his apprentices asked, he always managed to change the subject in such a way that you didn't notice until afterwards.

Hugh didn't stand a chance in a fight against Rhodes- he hadn't even when all Rhodes knew was a few basic cantrips. His new master should already be guiding him through attuning, so Rhodes likely had much more powerful magic available to him now, while Hugh had really only gotten better at wards. If he'd had a few seconds he could have drawn a ward, but without any time to prepare…

"Don't just stand there like one of your sheep, sheepherder. Tell us about your new affinity," said Rhodes.

The twins had spread out to either side of Hugh. He could tell that things were going to progress to a beating here in a moment. He could hear his heart pounding in his ears as it started beating faster.

"Don't just stand there like a lump, sheepherder," Rhodes said. He reached out towards Hugh, and then just… stopped. His face turned pale, and then he grabbed his crotch with both hands and dropped to the ground. Behind him, pulling back her foot, was Talia. Sabae stood just behind her.

"Hugh's no sheepherder," Talia said.

Hugh felt his mouth drop open in shock.

"You bitch!" growled Rhodes, slowly picking himself up from the ground and holding himself. "Do you know who I am?"

"You're the spoiled brat who's messing with our friend," Talia said. "Do you know who I am?"

One of the twins- the boy- finally spoke up.

"You're that barbarian bitch who can't control her magic at all," he said.

"And you're the useless storm mage whose family didn't want her anymore," said the girl.

Sabae's normally impassive face broke out in a scowl. She opened her mouth to say something, but Talia spoke first.

76

"I do know who you are, Charax," she said to Rhodes. "I am Talia of Clan Castis."

Rhodes' face grew red. Talia chuckled.

"I remember the story of when Highvale decided they'd had enough of our raids, and sent an army to try and punish us a century or so ago. Five thousand warriors and two hundred battle mages, and we caught them in a valley and incinerated them. It only took a hundred of us, and not a single Highvale soldier survived. We didn't lose a single warrior." Talia smiled even more broadly. "And they were lead by the then Crown Prince of Highvale. Your ancestor, I believe."

Rhodes bellowed wordlessly, pain forgotten. He brought his hand forward in a classic battlecasting pose, and sparks of lightning began to crackle around his fingers. Hugh flinched, ready to throw himself to the ground.

And then Sabae punched Rhodes so hard he went flying. A gust of wind blasted out of her closed fist as it struck his chest, and he was launched into the boy twin. Both of them were sent sliding a good twenty-five feet down the smooth stone floor, and Rhodes' lightning dissolved into harmless sparks. Hugh and the girl twin were knocked down to the ground by the wind as well.

Talia ran over to Hugh and hauled him up by his hand. Sabae was staring at her fist in shock. Talia dragged Hugh past Sabae, and yelled "Don't stick around after tweaking a dragon's tail, Sabae!" Sabae blinked, and turned to follow Hugh and Talia.

Hugh glanced back, and saw Rhodes glaring at them. Hugh had just been a petty amusement for the nobleman before, but the look he was giving them now? It was pure hate.

They ran through the hallways for several minutes before stopping to rest. Alustin's training programs were already showing their worth- before, Hugh doubted he could have run half as far.

After she'd caught her breath, Talia burst out laughing. "The looks on their faces! The look on your face, Sabae! That was amazing."

Hugh nodded in agreement. His heart was still racing, but not just from the run.

Sabae looked at them for a moment, then laughed. "I suppose Alustin's training programs actually are working, aren't they?"

"I thought you couldn't do magic at a distance?" Talia said.

"I wasn't. I just built up the wind around my fist and released it when I struck, and it just… naturally flowed in the direction of the strike. Before, it would have dispersed wildly in all directions," Sabae said. "This time, it just… followed the strike."

Talia and Sabae chuckled for a few moments, and then Sabae frowned and turned towards Hugh. Hugh still felt sick to the stomach from the encounter.

"This isn't the first time, is it?" Sabae said.

Hugh looked down at his feet. His cheeks flushed and his stomach began to twist itself back up again. They'd seen how much of a coward he was, and they'd want nothing to do with him now.

"No," he said in a quiet voice.

No one said anything for a moment, then Talia spoke up. "That pampered little bastard. Why didn't you tell us, Hugh? We'd have had your back in a heartbeat."

Hugh didn't say anything for a moment, then finally

worked up the nerve to speak, though even quieter than before. "I didn't want you to see how much of a coward I am," he said.

He didn't want to look up, but all of a sudden Sabae stepped up to him and grabbed his shoulders.

"Rhodes Charax is half again your size, has probably had combat training from the time he could walk, has multiple attunements, none of your disadvantages, is being trained by Aedan Dragonslayer himself, and had two friends at his back. If I know his type, he probably had friends when he did this before, too. Fighting him on your own would have been foolishness, not courage."

Hugh stared at her in the eyes for a moment. She seemed absolutely serious. He grew uncomfortable at her unblinking stare and turned his gaze towards Talia. Talia had an angry look on her face.

"If anything, Rhodes is the coward," Talia said. "With all the advantages he has, he still only faced you with backup."

Sabae nodded, and seeing that Hugh looked uncomfortable, let go of his shoulders. "We were walking to lunch when we ran across you, would you care to join us?"

Hugh just nodded, not trusting himself to speak. They set off towards the dining hall- the larger, student dining hall that Hugh had avoided for weeks. Talia and Sabae talked about the blow she'd struck as they walked, Hugh walking behind them. Talia wanted to call it a gust punch, while Sabae wanted to call it a wind strike.

After a couple of minutes, Hugh worked up the nerve to speak again. "Talia, did… did you mean it when you called me your friend?"

Both of the girls turned their heads back to look at

him.

"Of course you're our friend, Hugh," said Sabae. "Why would you think otherwise?"

Talia's face had resumed its customary furious look. "Because he's an idiot, that's why! How dumb do you have to be to not realize you're friends with someone! If I…"

As Talia ranted at him, Hugh felt a small smile creeping across his face. It wasn't as big as his earlier smile, but it felt much, much better.

CHAPTER EIGHT
Lunch

Talia, Sabae, and Hugh had just gotten their food when someone called Sabae's name. Hugh looked over to see a huge, muscular teen with curly black hair and skin darker than Sabae's waving at them. It took him a second, but then he recognized him as Artur Wallbreaker's son and apprentice. Sabae waved back, then headed over to the burly teen's table. Hugh paused uncertainly, but followed after Talia walked that way as well.

"Hugh, Talia, this is Godrick, son of Artur Wallbreaker. Godrick, this is Hugh of Emblin and Talia of Clan Castis." Sabae sat next to Godrick, while Hugh and Talia sat across the table from them.

"It's great ta meet yeh," said Godrick in a slightly too loud voice and a thick accent that Hugh couldn't place, and reached across the table to shake Talia's hand. Hugh, not wanting to be rude, followed suit, and regretted it immediately. It was like shaking hands with a bear. His hand *hurt* after that squeeze. He didn't think Godrick had squeezed so hard on purpose, though- he was immediately obvious as one of those people who didn't have a mean bone in his body, or even a less than joyously friendly bone.

Hugh thought people that friendly were exhausting.

"Sabae's told me a bit about the two a' yeh, but she won't tell me what yer affinities are. She told me ah've got to ask you if I want ta know," Godrick said. "Mine are pretty close ta me da's- Ah've got stone just like him, but with steel instead a' iron."

"What's the difference?" Talia asked.

"Iron mages can affect any iron an' iron alloys they want, steel mages can only affect steel with any real strength," Godrick said.

"So a steel attunement is just weaker than an iron attunement?" Talia said.

Godrick didn't seem at all offended. "Not at all- it's quite stronger, in fact. It's the way things work with similar attunements- the more specific the attunement is, the more powerful it tends ta be, at the cost of versatility. Ah might not be able to affect regular iron more than a tiny bit, and my da's iron not at all, but he can hardly touch my steel directly with his power, and he's miles ahead a' me. Doesn't matter too much, since ah'm mostly just usin' it to make mah hammer hit harder."

He leaned forwards. "It's a bit a' a secret, but since we're all friends here, I'll tell you something else, too."

Wait, friends? Hugh had just met the guy.

"We just met you," Talia said. She'd apparently been thinking along the same lines as Hugh.

Godrick waved his hand dismissively. "Any friend a' Sabae is a friend a' mine. 'sides, if ah wanted to hear your secrets, gotta offer something of mah own, right?"

Hugh wasn't sure what to say to that, so he kept to his usual strategy of not saying anything.

Godrick leaned forwards towards Hugh and Talia and dropped his voice to a whisper. "Ah've got a third affinity as well. Just a weak one, but it's a good 'un." He smiled broadly. "Scent."

Hugh blinked. Scent? How was that…

Talia whistled. "You're a stink mage? Remind me never to kick you in the britches."

Hugh shot Talia a confused look.

She caught it and explained. "There are only a couple Clans that Clan Castis avoids fighting. One of them, Clan Derem, specializes in scent mages. Their villages are the most wonderful smelling places on the planet, but get into a fight with Clan Derem? A stink mage can have a whole raiding party vomiting in seconds, and making skunks smell sweet compared to them for weeks."

Godrick chuckled. "Ah doubt ah'll ever be that powerful, but ah can sure give someone a bad day or two. And against monsters with powerful noses? Ah can give them a really bad day." He grinned even wider. "And ah can do this."

Hugh sensed a brief surge of mana coming from Godrick, and all of a sudden his relatively bland smelling soup smelled absolutely heavenly, and he was reminded how hungry he was. He tucked into the soup with a vengeance. The flavor didn't quite match the scent, but it was definitely improved from normal.

Maybe Godrick was alright after all.

"Ah also get a much better sense a' smell out a' the deal, which is nice. Can track by scent a bit," Godrick said, before tucking into his soup as well.

Talia gave him a considering look, then gave Godrick an abbreviated explanation of her affinities, tattoos, and training. When she mentioned manifesting dreamfire, his eyes widened.

"That's a crazy difficult skill ta' master! From what ah hear, most dream mages can't even attempt manifesting dreams before they're journeymen."

Talia grinned. "I've already done it."

It was Godrick's turn to whistle.

Hugh heard a faint sound and looked to Sabae. She was pursing her lips as though she were trying to whistle, but she was failing miserably. Sabae saw Hugh looking and quickly put her normal reserved look back on her face, but he could see her blushing a little.

"What about yerself, Hugh?" Godrick said.

Hugh jumped a little.

"Hugh's situation is… a little sensitive," Sabae said.

Godrick looked curiously between Hugh and Sabae. "Can't he tell me on his own?" He didn't sound offended, just curious.

"Good luck with that," Talia said. "We're his friends, and we can barely pry two words out of his mouth. Shyest kid I've ever met."

Hugh, feeling surprisingly ornery at that, spoke up. "Two words."

Everyone stared at him for a second, then Godrick burst out laughing. His laugh was as huge as the rest of him. Sabae quickly followed suit, while Talia just glared at Hugh. Hugh just looked down at his food and smiled.

"Nah worries if yeh don't feel like talking, Hugh. No debt, mah story was freely given ta yeh."

Godrick smiled broadly at Hugh, and turned to talk to Sabae about their combat training under his father.

Hugh sat quietly for a couple minutes eating his soup. When a lull in the conversation finally occurred, he spoke up. "I don't have any affinities."

Godrick blinked, and for the first time in the conversation, looked like he didn't know what to say.

"Not yet," Hugh said, and looked back to his food.

Godrick finally got his mouth working. "That's a cryptic statement if ah ever heard one." When it became apparent that Hugh didn't intend to say any more, he grinned. "Ah like a good puzzle."

Talia elbowed Hugh in the side. He looked at her, startled and a little offended.

"Look who's in line," she said.

Hugh looked up and spotted Rhodes in line glaring at them. The twins were there as well, but their glares paled besides the hate in Rhodes' eyes.

Godrick whistled again. "There's an angry fella. What did yeh three do ta make him mad like that?"

Sabae quit trying- and failing- to copy Godrick's whistle again. "Talia kicked him in the fork," she said.

Almost at the same time, Talia said "Sabae hit him with a gust punch so hard he and his goons there went flying."

Sabae gave Talia a dirty look. "Wind strike."

"Gust punch."

"Wind stri…"

"Gust strike," Hugh interrupted.

Godrick stared at the three of them in shock, then burst out laughing, this time so loud that a number of students around the dining hall looked at them. Rhodes turned bright red.

"Ah don't know tha Winter twins too well, but that Rhodes is a' prideful fella. He wasn't real happy when ah turned down his invitation ta join his labyrinth team. Didn't want to join someone who seemed ta take it fer granted ah'd do so."

Hugh looked at Godrick in confusion.

"The team yer supposed ta assemble fer tha first year final?" Godrick said, catching Hugh's look.

Hugh just shrugged.

"First years delve into the Labyrinth below Skyhold for their final at the summer solstice," Sabae said. "They're only permitted to explore the first level, which is fairly safe. Most students come back. You need to do it in teams of four, though, just in case."

This did not especially comfort Hugh. The Labyrinth was hellishly dangerous, everyone knew that. Even ignoring the monsters and traps, the maze itself changed its shape regularly.

Godrick had a thoughtful look on his face. "Ye know, there are four a' us…"

Talia gave him a glare. "You've been planning to ask us that since we got here, haven't you?"

"Guilty," Godrick said with a grin.

"Sounds good to me," Sabae said.

Talia gave Godrick an appraising look, then snorted. "You look like you can handle yourself in a fight, and failing that you can carry us if we get tired. Fine by me."

Everyone looked at Hugh expectantly. He hunched down a little at the attention, but then sighed. "That'd be fine, I guess."

Godrick seemed to take that as words of the highest praise, and clapped Hugh on the shoulder while smiling broader than ever. "Ah knew ye'd come around, bud. We still need ta ask me da and yer master, but ah reckon they'll be fine with it."

Hugh rubbed his shoulder ruefully. He was fairly sure he was going to bruise.

CHAPTER NINE

Spellform

Hugh's routine changed quite a bit after that. Godrick started joining them for many of their morning exercise sessions, as did his father. Artur Wallbreaker was even bigger up close than Hugh had expected, both in sheer physical size and personality. He made Godrick seem quiet and demure at times. His hair and beard- both immense in size- were shot through with strands of white, and he had more scars over his bulging muscles than Hugh could count. He was, if anything, even friendlier than Godrick.

Most of the rest of the day went the same until lunch. Alustin's three apprentices (though not Godrick, who ate lunch at a different time) talked much more than they used to. Even Hugh started talking a bit more often as he grew comfortable with the others.

During the later part of the afternoon, as they trained in magic, Talia and Sabae showed immense progress.

Talia could now consistently manifest dreamfire, and even hurl fist-sized bursts of it at targets with a fair degree of accuracy. Dreamfire, disturbingly, didn't always burn its target, but always damaged it somehow. Sometimes the target would be frozen solid, other times aged until it crumpled to dust, or on one memorable occasion, diced into hundreds of perfect half inch cubes. Still, three out of every four times, dreamfire behaved mostly like real fire. Alustin still hadn't figured a way to develop Talia's bone affinity yet, unfortunately.

Sabae had shown massive improvement, at least with her wind attunement. She could regularly release gust strikes with her blows now. She had begun the rudiments of developing it into wind armor- she could now manifest bracers of swirling wind around her forearms that resembled faint tornadoes. They couldn't deflect a lot, and Sabae could only maintain them a few seconds at a time with the current size of her mana reservoirs, but they were enough to significantly cushion most blows. Alustin still cautioned her against using her water or lightning affinities, and Sabae still refused to use her healing affinity.

Hugh's list of potential contract partners had grown- Chelys Mot the earthquake tortoise, Lasnabourne the phoenix, and a sentient, plant controlling tree in the same archipelago as Lasnabourne were all new additions approved by Alustin.

Hugh, however, hadn't cast a single spell other than his wards and his basic light spell. He'd learned why the light spell worked- unlike most other cantrips, it was built to accept a highly variable amount of mana, so that its relative brightness could be adjusted easily enough. It had been much more capable of accepting the huge amounts of mana he couldn't help but dump into every spell.

All Hugh did was just keep learning more and more about spellform construction. He learned what the various basic shapes did, how they relate to one another, and how the speed and turbulence of mana flows were affected as they went through turns and intersections at different angles. But Alustin still didn't teach him to cast any spells.

He often found himself extremely frustrated by the end of magic training, but he still always found himself looking forwards to dinner. He always ate with Talia and Sabae, and Godrick managed to make it most nights as well. He always enjoyed himself, and found himself contributing more and more often to the conversation-though no one would be quick to accuse him of being talkative.

Rhodes never did anything, but Hugh noticed that very few students were willing to sit near the four of them. Hugh guessed Rhodes had made his dislike of them known to their peers.

It was his lack of progress at magic, however, that really began to grate at him.

Finally, about three weeks after the confrontation with Rhodes and meeting Godrick, he reached a breaking point in Alustin's office. Sabae was off doing combat training, while Talia had been sent to the library to retrieve a number of books, including a rare biography of an Ithonian Empire dream mage.

"Why haven't you taught me any spells yet?" Hugh demanded of Alustin.

Alustin quirked his eyebrow at Hugh. "I thought that's what I've been doing."

"You haven't yet, though!" Hugh said. "I don't know any new spells outside of my wards."

Alustin seemed to consider for a moment, then nodded. "I definitely have been teaching you new spells, you just haven't been listening."

Hugh spluttered for a moment, but Alustin cut him off.

"What did I tell you I'd be teaching you at the very beginning, Hugh?"

"How to adjust spells to work for me, and how to improvise my own spells" Hugh said.

"Exactly. I don't believe I ever told you I'd be teaching you spells on their own. The whole point of learning spellform construction is that so you can craft your own." Alustin grabbed a sheet of paper and a quill, handing them to Hugh.

"You're going to craft a levitation spell to lift this book."

Hugh glared at Alustin, then at the book he'd set in front of Hugh. "How am I supposed to do that?"

"Draw a foundation for your spellform."

Hugh paused for a moment, then started sketching. The foundation was the most critical part of any spellform- it was what channeled the caster's mana into the rest of it. Hugh chose to go with a high capacity, octagonal foundation line.

"Now draw your definitive lines." These lines were what guided the mana into the form it needed to be- in this case, the skewed diagonals he drew were what told the spell that it was supposed to bestow kinetic energy onto its target.

"Now draw your aiming lines." These short, branching lines coming off the definitive lines told the spell what direction the kinetic energy should be applied towards.

Alustin leaned back in his chair. "Now use it."

Hugh carefully memorized the diagram he'd drawn, then focused on the book. He drew the octagon in his mind's eye, followed by the skewed diagonals, followed by the branching aiming lines. Targeting the spell was done by application of the caster's will- everyone, apparently, invested at least a little bit of willforce into all their spells, though few could invest as much as Hugh

89

could into his wards. Finally, he carefully let his mana flow into the spellform.

The book launched itself upwards from the desk at high speeds, slamming into the ceiling. Hugh stopped channeling mana into the spellform at the loud bang, and the book promptly crashed back onto the desk, bending a few of the pages.

Hugh felt himself turn red. "It still didn't work right! This has all been a waste of time!"

Alustin picked up the book and smoothed out the pages. "It levitated, didn't it?"

"Sure, but it didn't stop when it was supposed to!" Hugh said.

Alustin grabbed another sheet of paper, and swiftly drew out another spellform- it had the same definitive lines and similar aiming lines, but a very different foundation line.

"This is the standard basic levitation spellform," Alustin said. "All it has is the foundation line, the definitive lines, and the aiming lines. What happens when you try to use it?"

Hugh glared sullenly. "It explodes, or releases a flash of light, or it smokes a bunch."

"And what's the difference between the two spellforms?" Alustin held them up side by side.

"The foundation line on the standard spellform is built to only handle a little bit of mana- considerably less than I put into it," Hugh said.

"Which is why it reacts so badly- the mana you channel into the spellform is too much for it, and it shatters the spellform," Alustin said. "Your new spellform, however, did not shatter, since you gave it the capacity to handle your mana."

"So why did it fail?" Hugh said.

"It didn't. Try it again."

Hugh gave Alustin a skeptical look, but recreated the spellform. Once again the book launched itself to the ceiling, startling Hugh into releasing the spell.

"Again, but this time don't lose concentration when it hits the ceiling."

Hugh tried a third time. He carefully recreated the spellform in his mind, took a deep breath, and then channeled his mana into it. The book shot upwards, but this time, Hugh managed to avoid losing the spell. After the book hit, it just… stayed there, stuck to the ceiling.

"Unlike the standard spells, you're not getting random, chaotic results, because you're not shattering the spellform," Alustin said. "The standard levitation spell only lifts small objects a couple of feet because that's all the mana the foundation line channels into the effect. Your spellform, however, can channel enough mana to lift this book… around twenty or thirty feet, I'd wager."

The book, which had remained pinned against the ceiling, abruptly shot off along the ceiling to one side, slamming against the office door. Hugh lost concentration in surprise.

"Your aiming lines weren't the best, unfortunately- the aiming lines in the standard levitation spell horizontally stabilize the levitated object, whereas your spell allows it to transfer its vertical force into horizontal force. It likely would have launched the book off to the side as well if it had managed to actually lift the book all the way to the top of your spell."

Hugh stared at the book for a moment.

"If you'd wanted to reduce the height the book rose to, there are a couple of ways to do that," Alustin said. "What is known as a restrictor line can be applied to the aiming line to limit the top of the effect. A venting line can be added to the foundation line to release any mana over a certain amount before it becomes part of the spell. Additional definitive lines could be added to the spell- say, light lines to make the book glow- in order to use up more of the mana so the book wouldn't have launched itself so high."

Alustin paused and looked at Hugh straight in the eye.

"You're going to learn about all of these and more, and they'll all give you much, much greater versatility with your spells. You could have been creating spellforms of your own for a few weeks, now, though. You should have figured that out by now, Hugh. You can't expect your teachers- even me- to just hand you everything. You need to learn to find your own answers as well. But…" Alustin smiled broadly, "I'm happy to congratulate you for creating your first original spell. You've already achieved something that many mages never even attempt in their entire careers."

Hugh blinked, then smiled.

Just then, however, Talia entered the office and promptly tripped over the book Hugh had been levitating, sending her armful of books tumbling across the floor.

"What idiot just left a book right in the entryway? Were you trying to break someone's neck?" Talia sounded like she was prepared to rant for quite a long time. Hugh's smile turned a little sheepish, and he got out of his chair to go help Talia pick up her books.

Hugh spent the next few days levitating things constantly. He found out a few things pretty quickly.

First off, while his friends were excited for Hugh, they were less appreciative of having their stuff launched across a room.

Second, that spellform crafting was far, far more daunting of a task than he'd appreciated. His first attempt to alter the aiming lines so that the target of his spell wasn't launched off to one side resulted in the spell trying to crumple the levitated object. He'd tried to simply use the aiming lines from the standard levitation spell, but it was far from that simple- it turned out that the different foundation line changed the requirements for the aiming line. So he had to figure out how to adjust the aiming lines appropriately.

When he tried it again, it didn't try to crumple the levitated object, but it did spin it at a high speed. It seemed that the changes to the aiming lines necessitated that they be moved slightly farther down the definitive lines, which in turn…

Hugh quickly started realizing why so few mages tried to learn spellform construction, and he started to seriously question the sanity of trying to master the skill of doing it on the fly.

He did a little research, and found that the average mage generally memorized a dozen or fewer spells- there was a reason most mages carried spellbooks filled with different spellforms and their descriptions. In order to cast a spell they didn't have memorized, they had to sort through their spellbooks to find the spellform. Not very useful in battle, though most mages weren't battlemages.

So being able to construct spells on the fly had some pretty clear advantages in versatility. Still, the sheer difficulty of doing the task was daunting- most spellform crafters didn't even try, instead creating new spells in shielded labs in case they went wrong, carefully testing and preparing them before selling them.

Alustin apparently expected far, far more from Hugh than he'd ever realized.

Hugh also looked a bit into enchanting- there was definitely quite a bit of overlap between the two. Enchanting, however, was a whole different kind of complication, because the runes and glyphs used in enchanting were a specialized type of spellform designed to work on a physical object, rather than via a mage- glyph and rune spellforms had to be drawn very, very differently. Not to mention the mana conducting tolerances of the materials being crafted had to be factored into their crafting, and…

Enchanting looked fascinating, but Hugh wanted to stick to trying to master just one discipline absurdly beyond his skill level for now.

Still, these experiments with his levitation spell alone showed Hugh exactly how far he had to go, and he redoubled his efforts at his studies. One major concern, however, was that he was learning spellform crafting at the cantrip stage, rather than as a fully attuned mage- he wasn't sure if there would be any important differences between the two.

Alustin, when asked, laughed. "I was wondering when you'd ask that! The answer is no- even most high level spells involve quite a bit of unattuned mana, and cantrips aren't actually entirely unattuned. Your basic levitation spell uses mana tinged with gravity and force attunements, and your basic fire starting spell uses fire tinged mana."

"So what's the point of attunements, then?" Hugh said.

"The simplest answer is that without attunements," Alustin said, "you can only provide slightly attuned mana to a spell, not the deeply attuned mana that spellforms for deep attunements need. You can use unattuned mana to light tinder for a campfire, but you can't throw a fireball with it."

"So developing my spellcrafting now…"

"Will most certainly apply after you contract with a magical entity and attune, yes. Speaking of which, do you have any more candidates for us to look at?"

CHAPTER TEN

The Lair Revealed

Hugh carefully added the last restriction line to the spellform in his mind's eye, and oh so carefully channeled the mana into it, and… He held his breath as the head sized stone sphere, covered in chalk markings, hovered up into the air about three feet.

"Yes!" he said.

Talia rolled her eyes. "You levitated another rock. We've seen you do it a thousand times at this point."

Hugh grinned. "Throw some dreamfire at it."

Talia gave him a skeptical look. They were in one of the student practice chambers. Talia was taking a break from her training to refill her mana reservoirs, while Godrick and Sabae sparred on the other side of the room.

"Why would I do that?" Talia asked.

"Just try it," Hugh insisted with a grin.

Talia rolled her eyes at him, but stood up. Almost leisurely, she lobbed a fist size ball of dreamfire at the sphere.

The sphere dodged upwards, letting the fireball pass below it. The dreamfire slammed against the stone walls of the room, which were enchanted to prevent damage from spells- at least any spells students could cast.

Talia narrowed her eyes, then glared at Hugh.

"So you made a spell that lets you personally control the height of the sphere? You could have practiced that without bugging me."

Hugh grinned. "Nope. Try again."

Talia launched another fireball, and the sphere dodged to the left, narrowly avoiding being hit. Talia glared at it, then launched a pair of fist sized fireballs- one straight at it, one above it.

The sphere dodged downwards.

Talia growled, then let loose a veritable storm of projectiles.

The sphere dodged every single one, never moving more than a foot from its original location.

At this point, Godrick and Sabae had stopped sparring to watch. Talia was actually working up a sweat, and her rate of fire had dropped significantly. Finally she stopped and whirled on Hugh.

"What did you do to that thing? It's jumping like a man who just fell in a snowmelt stream."

Hugh grinned even wider, then hurled an acorn sized pebble at the sphere. It hit the sphere without the sphere trying to dodge at all. "I warded it. Whenever the ward detects dream mana approaching it, it sends out a directional mana pulse. Then I created a levitation spell set to react to those pulses, so that the sphere dodges dreamfire accordingly. The spell then brings the sphere back to the midpoint."

Talia stared at him again, then turned to face the

sphere again. She launched a single dreamfire bolt at the sphere. Hugh watched smugly, convinced that there was no way she'd hit.

The dreamfire bolt headed straight for the sphere. It swiftly dodged out of the way, only for the dreamfire bolt to simply… stop. It hung in midair, right at the centerpoint where the sphere usually hung. The sphere, having completed its outward movement, simply swung back into the center. Right into the hanging dreamfire.

Hugh's jaw dropped as he watched a chunk of the stone sphere seem to sprout into vines and then wither away, leaving a fist sized hole in the sphere. Talia grinned, then launched several more dreamfire bolts at the sphere.

All of them hit. The ward spellform Hugh had drawn on it in had been broken by the first bolt, so it was no longer sending out the directional pulses. With a slightly embarrassed look, Hugh stopped channeling mana into the spell, and the broken remains of the sphere dropped to the ground.

"Nice try, Hugh," Talia said, grinning.

Hugh sighed, then went back to his assigned practice. He was supposed to be combining multiple basic cantrip effects into a single spellform. Thus far he'd topped out at three- he could levitate an item, make it glow, and make it emit a noise. He hadn't managed any other combination of cantrip effects, however.

It'd been weeks since he'd successfully cast his first levitation spell. At this point, he could replicate all of the basic cantrips students were expected to know at will, as well as doing a lot of basic modifications of them on the fly.

Which, given the limited power of cantrips, left him

functionally months behind most of the other students. Until he got a warlock contract with a decently powerful magical entity, he wouldn't be able to really start catching up with the other students. Everyone else at this point was already well on their way into learning to attune.

Hugh was getting more and more stressed out as the labyrinth test approached. Admittedly, everyone else was stressing out about it as well, but at least everyone else on the team had real magic to contribute.

Still, even with that stress hanging over his head, Hugh was happier than he could ever remember being since his parents had died.

He'd shared the full details of his mage situation and being a warlock with Godrick eventually, and much to his surprise, Godrick found the whole thing extremely exciting. He'd actually started helping Hugh find possible contract partners. He hadn't told Godrick much about the rest of his past, but Godrick seemed to respect his privacy. He wasn't sure how much the others had told Godrick about their stories.

Hugh found himself spending less and less time in his hidden lair, which he still hadn't told anyone about, and more and more time with Talia, Sabae, and Godrick. The four trained together for the labyrinth daily now, and many of their reading assignments were now on the nature of the labyrinth, accounts of the inside, and dangers commonly found there.

Rhodes hadn't tried anything in weeks, which was a lovely change as well. Of course, Hugh was seldom alone and vulnerable anymore.

It was on a Fourthday evening after dinner that Hugh's

lair was discovered. He'd split ways with the others after dinner and doubled back into the library, declining Godrick's invitation to the group to spend the evening out on one of the balconies watching sandships dock.

Hugh had taken his usual convoluted route back to his lair, dodging past origami golems and librarians, but to his later chagrin, wasn't paying that much attention to his surroundings. He ducked behind the bookshelf his door lay behind- the contents of which he'd replaced with dull accounts of tax law and defunct trade agreements, to further disinterest passerby in looking at his shelf- and through his heavily warded door.

He'd sat down at his desk to start working on his newest projects when his alarm wards went off, making his glow crystals start flashing off and on. There was a loud banging noise as some of the more active wards went off, and someone started cursing.

Hugh realized that someone had followed him back to his room and panicked. His wards were set to go off if someone tried to open his door. It must have been Rhodes. He'd just been biding his time, waiting for Hugh to be alone and inattentive.

Hugh scrambled for the window, considering trying to climb outside. He hadn't even opened it more than partway when he remembered that his window opened onto a sheer rock face. He panicked, frantically looking around his room for some way to escape, when he recognized the cursing outside.

Hugh sighed. He was still shaking a bit, but walked open to the door and opened it. "Talia."

Talia glared at him. She was lying on top of the bookshelf that had hidden his door, which had been knocked over by his wards going off. She was bleeding pretty badly from a cut over her eye, and it looked like she'd have quite a few nasty bruises soon.

He reached down to help her up, and she smacked his hand away.

"This is how you greet a friend, is it?" she demanded.

"I... I didn't know you were coming," Hugh said.

"No, because you never trusted us enough to tell us where you live," Talia snapped. Her face was growing red with anger.

She'd risen up onto her feet, and looked like she wanted to punch him. Hugh's stomach curdled a little bit. It wasn't that he didn't trust his friends, he'd just somehow never gotten around to telling them about his room. It was a little paranoid, maybe, but it wasn't about them, he knew they would never...

"What are you just standing there like a great lump for? Not even going to apologize for almost killing me?"

Hugh tried to say something, but nothing came out of his mouth. Talia growled and shoved him. Hugh went toppling down to the ground.

"I thought we were friends," Talia said.

By the time he'd stood up, she was gone.

It took Hugh several hours to finish picking the bookshelf back up and re-shelve the books.

He spent a while trying to work on his new project, but couldn't keep focused. He switched over to trying to browse the Bestiary more, but eventually just gave up and went to bed after spending hours reading and rereading the entry on Kraggoth Claw-Mane, some sort of insane chimera imprisoned below the capital of the Havath Dominion.

He didn't even bother to take off his clothes when he

got in bed, and barely slept that night. He kept having nightmares about forming his pact with some sort of shadowy monster who demanded Hugh's friends as the price for his power.

Fifthday was even worse. A few times he tried to make himself leave his lair, but he never made it farther than a few dozen feet away before his heart would start racing and he felt like he needed to throw up. He didn't even go to the dining hall to get food- not, that is, that he felt hungry. He spent most of the day in bed, drifting in and out of shallow dozes. He only left to go to the restroom and drink water from the bathroom in the stacks- and even with how few people used it, he was still especially careful not to run into anyone.

The only thing that Hugh accomplished that day was rebuilding his wards. This time he made sure to build in exemptions for his friends.

If Talia even wanted to be his friend anymore.

He'd finally made his first friends and now he'd ruined it. Talia wouldn't want to see him anymore and everyone else would take her side and…

Part of Hugh knew that his anxieties were completely unjustified. Talia dealt with her problems head on, she didn't scheme or gossip. She'd most likely just tell everyone else she got in a fight.

Most of Hugh, however, was more than ready to believe the worst, no matter how ridiculous.

Hugh didn't dream that night.

On Sixthday morning, Hugh sat on his floor under the window, knees under his chin, staring at the door. He'd turned down his glowcrystals and closed his curtain, so his room was dark as night. He knew he should get out of bed and go to morning training, but the thought of leaving his room was entirely too much for him. He just kept replaying the conversation with Talia in his head, cursing himself for being so incompetent with other people. Classtime eventually came and went, as did lunch.

Hugh had just slipped back into a light sleep, still sitting under the window, when someone knocked on his door. His eyes shot open, and his heart started pounding a mile a minute. He didn't move. Nothing else happened for a moment, and Hugh started to try and convince himself that it had just been a dream.

"I know you're in there, Hugh."

It was Talia.

Hugh opened his mouth to say something, but nothing came out.

"Hugh…"

He heard a light thunk on the door, like someone hitting their forehead against the wood.

"I'm sure you've upgraded your wards even more, and they'll blast me across the library this time, but I'm coming in."

Hugh's heart was hammering even harder.

The door opened. Talia was standing on the other side, arm shielding her face in preparation for a blast that never came. She had a bandage on her forehead, and several bruises on her arms. She slowly lowered her arm, and Hugh quickly looked at the floor so he wouldn't meet her gaze.

Talia stood in the doorway for a few moments, her eyes adjusting to the dim light that made it in past the bookshelf. After a few moments, she took a couple steps into the room.

"I built exemptions into the ward for you three this time," Hugh whispered.

He heard Talia sigh, then she turned up the glowcrystals in his room. He curled up a little more.

Talia shut the door, then slowly walked over to Hugh. She stood there silently for a minute, then lowered herself to a sitting position on the floor in front of him.

Neither said anything for a few minutes. Finally, Talia spoke up.

"I'm sorry, Hugh."

Hugh didn't say anything.

"It might have bugged me that you hid where you lived from us, but I should have talked to you instead of following you. I violated your privacy. I tried to open your door even though I knew how private you were and how good you were with wards. Then, rather than own up to my own idiocy, I got mad at you instead."

She didn't say anything for a moment.

"I calmed down and felt like an ass within the hour, but I was too embarrassed to come back here. I was completely convinced that you were probably furious at me, so I spent all of yesterday training and avoiding everyone. This morning, I had to drag myself to training, and when you weren't there… I felt awful. The others asked if I knew where you were, since they hadn't heard from you since Fourthday dinner."

Talia paused again.

"I was a coward and told them you hadn't been feeling well. They all bought it, except maybe Alustin, but he didn't say anything." She sighed. "I couldn't focus at all today. I slipped away after training was done to come talk to you, but I must have stood out there for an hour before I found the nerve to knock."

She didn't say anything for a few minutes, just sat there.

"Please say something, Hugh."

Hugh wanted to say something, but couldn't even manage to lift his head from behind his knees.

"You... you probably want me to leave. I'll... I'm sorry, I shouldn't have come." Talia stood up to leave. As she turned to go out the door, Hugh finally worked up the nerve to lift up his head and speak.

"Wait."

Talia stopped, and slowly turned around. Hugh stared at her for a moment, tears running down his cheeks, then looked back down at the ground.

"Don't go."

Talia stood there for a moment looking at him, then slowly walked over and slid down the wall to sit next to him. She wrapped her arm around him, and didn't say anything as he cried.

Hugh and Talia must have sat there quietly for at least an hour before he finally managed to get his thoughts in some form of order.

"I thought you didn't want to be friends anymore," he said weakly.

Talia glared at him. "Don't be an idiot, of course I...". She stopped midsentence and grinned, though there wasn't any real humor to it. "I came here to apologize, and end up yelling again. I'm really not the best at apologizing."

She squeezed him tight around the shoulders. "I was just angry and being a huge pile of goat droppings towards you. Of course I still want to be friends. If, that is, you still want to..."

Hugh nodded firmly, and Talia sighed in relief.

Neither of them spoke for a moment.

"Something in me's broken, Talia," he said. "I... can't stand up to Rhodes when he bullies me. I'm in constant terror that you three will stop wanting to be friends with me. We have one argument and I go almost catatonic for two days."

Talia started to say something, then paused. "Hugh, you don't have to answer if you don't want to, but... when you told us your story that day in the library, you left out Rhodes' bullying. Was there... was there more you were leaving out too?"

Hugh didn't move or say anything for a moment, and then nodded his head.

Talia's forehead wrinkled in concern. "Hugh, your aunt and uncle... no one... did anything... to you, you know..." She sounded extremely uncomfortable.

"Nothing like that," Hugh said. "No one ever... nothing like that." He took a deep, raggedy breath. "But it was a lot worse than I let on that day, yeah. And... I've never really had any friends before. I was always pretty shy and bad with people, even before..."

"Do you want to talk about it?" Talia said.

Hugh shook his head. "Not... not right now."

Hugh was happy when Talia pretended not to notice that he was crying again, but he was grateful when she squeezed him even harder in a hug.

Once Hugh had collected himself again, and wiped his face on his sleeve, he sat up a bit. He gave Talia a weak smile. "Would you like the tour?"

Talia grinned. "Sure."

Hugh pushed himself to his feet. "This over here is my bed. That's my desk, and over here," he said, pulling open his curtains, "is my window."

He popped the window panes open as well. Talia gasped. The sun was just going down on the horizon, and the dunes of the Endless Erg hand been painted in lurid sunset shades. A sandship was just pulling into Skyhold's port out of the Endless Erg, and a flock of drakes was playing in the air over it.

"Hugh… this is… this is…" Talia punched him in the shoulder.

"Ow! What was that for?" Hugh said.

"I'm jealous, this view is amazing! I doubt Rhodes even has a room with a window, let alone a view like this. How'd you find this place?"

Hugh told her the story of how he'd first met Alustin, then eventually found this room. He told her about the Choosing, and how he was sure that Alustin must have magicked in the bed somehow.

Then he showed her his new project. She grinned wickedly when she saw it. "Now that's going to come in handy during our labyrinth test." Hugh started to tell her more about it, only to be interrupted by his stomach growling.

"When's the last time you've eaten, Hugh?"

Hugh, embarrassed to say he hadn't eaten since before their fight, looked at the ground.

"The dining hall should still be open, if you want to join me," Talia said. "I haven't eaten anything since lunch, so I'm starving."

Hugh nodded.

Talia chuckled, and turned towards the door. She paused before going out, though. "You should get changed before we go. Don't take this the wrong way, but you smell really, really bad. I'll just wait outside your door for you."

She shut the door behind her.

Hugh sniffed at his shirt and winced.

CHAPTER ELEVEN

Birthday

Talia, to Hugh's gratitude, never told anyone about how she found his lair, and as far as anyone else was concerned, he'd just been sick.

He did, however, make sure to finally invite the others to visit his lair. It quickly became one of their favorite places to hang out. They smuggled several armchairs and a coffee table into his lair so there'd be enough room for everyone to fit, and Hugh often had to boot his friends off of his desk when he needed to do homework.

Hugh had thought it would be stressful to have that much less privacy, but it was actually really nice. He was able to relax in his room in a way he wasn't everywhere else.

He did, however, make sure to upgrade the wards to help keep noise coming from inside the room muted. Neither Godrick nor Talia was the best at the whole keeping quiet thing.

It was precisely two weeks before the summer solstice when Hugh got woken up by his friends all jumping on top of his bed. Thankfully, Godrick had the good sense not to jump on him, though Talia and Sabae were heavy enough.

"Happy birthday!" shouted the three together.

"Bwuh," was the most cogent thing Hugh could muster. He eventually managed to boot the three of them out of his room long enough for him to change, but they were back in the instant he was done.

"Presents!" said Talia, hurling a cloth wrapped bundle at Hugh. It bounced off his chest before he caught it. Whatever it was, it was metal and heavy for its size. He rubbed the spot on his chest where it had struck him before unwrapping it. Inside the bundle was a dagger in a leather sheath. The pommel of the dagger, decorated with patterns that resembled flames, had been what had struck him in the chest.

"Did ye just throw a knife at him?" Godrick asked, grinning. Talia kicked him in the shin.

"It's a Clan Castis dagger," Talia said. "It's not enchanted or anything, but it's well made and sturdy. And we only give them out to friends of the clan, so be careful with it!"

"I will," Hugh said, grinning.

Talia poked him hard in the stomach.

"Seriously, take care of it. You can show this knife to anyone in Clan Castis, and they'll be honor-bound to help you. Though you can expect a lot of questions about where you got it afterwards."

Hugh looked at the dagger, then bowed a little over it. "I'll take good care of it, Talia. This is a better gift than I deserve." She nodded, looking a little embarrassed.

"My turn," Sabae said, elbowing the other two aside. She handed Hugh her present. It was a paper wrapped bundle about the size of a pillow. Hugh started to tear it open, then grinned, picked up the knife Talia had given him, and used it to cut the package open.

Inside were two books. One was a thick, leatherbound

tome. Unlike Galvachren's Bestiary, however, it was still well within normal book size. There was an adjustable leather strap running from either end of the binding- the book was clearly meant to be worn over the shoulder. There was also a strap with a latch holding the book closed, which Hugh undid to reveal all blank pages. There were several quills and a couple sticks of drawing charcoal strapped inside one cover. A pocket sewn onto the shoulder strap turned out to have a compact inkpot stored in it.

"My family sent me this spellbook, but since I'm learning formless casting, it's not much use to me," Sabae said. "It's a lot bigger than normal spellbooks, so I figured it would be handy for you to take notes in and plan out spells."

Hugh grinned and flipped through its pages. A normal spellbook was small enough to fit in the pocket of a pair of trousers, and merely contained one or two spellform diagrams per page, with some details about each. It was meant to be used quickly. This book, however, would be absolutely perfect for planning out spells in detail.

He picked up the second book. This lizard-skin bound volume was small enough to fit in his trouser pockets- about the size of a more conventional spellbook. He flipped it open, expecting to see it blank, and instead was greeted with intricate and absurdly cramped handwriting and diagrams. As he browsed through it, he realized that the whole book was filled with notes about constructing wards on a massive scale- big enough to encompass a fortress or even a city.

He looked up in shock. "This is…"

Sabae was grinning. "That was my great-grandmother's notebook. She specialized in wards, and could build stormwards powerful enough to protect a ship at sea or even shield an entire city from a hurricane."

"I can't take this," Hugh said. "This sort of thing is priceless."

"My family has already made copies of it, so they were happy to send it when I asked them to. They also told me to tell you that if you ever get good enough to make wards like this, you've always got a job with them."

Hugh swallowed, not knowing what to say. Sabae grinned, and gave him a hug.

When she stepped back, Talia elbowed her in the side. "Of course you've got to go and one-up me with a better present. Now I just have to hope Godrick one-ups you."

Godrick looked a little embarrassed to hand Hugh his present. "Ah didn't even wrap mine."

Godrick's present was a hollow glass marble. The glass was clear and etched with complex spellforms.

"Ah managed ta convince one of tha enchanting instructors ta help me make it in exchange for helping him make himself one. Only worked thanks to mah scent attunment."

"What does it do?" Sabae asked. Hugh had been trying to puzzle out the spellforms etched into the marble himself, but they were fiendishly complex, and considerably different than the spellforms he was familiar with.

"It eats scents," Godrick said. "Rub it in yer armpits and it'll... eat the scent, make ye smell better."

Hugh blushed a little, but grinned. He definitely had a little bit of an issue with getting a bit ripe-smelling, so this would be incredibly handy.

Talia hugged Godrick. "Definitely my favorite present Hugh's gotten today."

Hugh grinned and made a rude gesture at Talia, but hugged Godrick as well.

Then something occurred to him. "Wait, how did you know it was my birthday today? I don't think I ever told you all about it."

"Alustin told us," Sabae said.

Of course he had.

"So we were planning to drag you to breakfast and then go spend the day watching sandships at the port, if you were interested," Sabae said.

That did sound pretty fun to Hugh. He hadn't been back down to the port since he'd arrived at Skyhold. But…

"That does sound fun, but I have a better idea."

"Are ye sure this is ah good idea?" Godrick asked again. Despite his formidable size, he was by far the most nervous of the four of them.

"Nope, but it's a fun one!" Talia said.

Hugh rolled his eyes. "It'll be fine, Godrick."

Hugh, in his explorations of the stacks, had discovered something interesting- a door leading into the deeper levels of the library, the ones far below the levels Alustin had given them permission to enter. To the levels that were forbidden to students. Though, really, the door wasn't the interesting part- there were a large number of doors in the stacks that led to those levels. What made this door interesting was that it had apparently been forgotten about by the library staff, and the wards on it allowed to slowly decay.

The fact that the door was on the lowest, most dimly lit level in the stacks, in the back of a store-room packed close to the ceiling with books, the entrance itself of which was partially hidden behind another shelf probably contributed to it being forgotten. They actually had to climb over the crates full of old textbooks and the like to get to the door. Hugh was surprised he'd found it in the first place, even given all the hours he spent exploring the stacks. He'd just trusted his gut.

With all the time Hugh had spent practicing his wards, he'd picked up a decent bit about ward-breaking as well. In retrospect, all that Rhodes had probably needed to disrupt the wards on his old room was simply a sharp knife to cut the design, along with a simple spell disruption cantrip. Wardbreaking wasn't nearly so difficult as their instructors had let on at first.

That is, at least for basic wards. This ward was a different beast entirely. If it hadn't been ignored and decaying for decades, there was no way Hugh could have attempted to break it. It was hellishly more complex than anything Hugh had ever attempted himself. Instead of the simple chalk he used for his wards, it was worked into a brass band set into the floor in front of the door. And instead of just being a one-off defense, it had multiple layers- a permanent physical shield, among others.

Hugh carefully sketched the ward patterns on the first pages of his new spellbook as the others watched. It was, Hugh thought, a pretty fitting first thing to draw in his new notebook.

The others had been surprisingly patient so far, just sitting on the piles of books filling the storeroom. Well, Sabae being patient wasn't a surprise, but Talia being patient definitely was.

Hugh grinned. The ward had looked nauseatingly complex at first, but at its base it operated the same as any of the wards Hugh had ever drawn- a sequence of spellforms bound together in a sequence, with conditions outlined in the spellforms that would detail when the ward would be activated and what effects would result. If Hugh tried to simply sever the ward, it would be set off.

On the other hand, if Hugh was careful, he could certainly modify the conditions for setting off the ward.

Hugh gave his diagrams in his new journal one last careful look and pulled a stick of chalk out of his pocket. He carefully set to work on the ward.

"Are you supposed to be drawing off of the brass, Hugh?" Talia said. "Doesn't seem like a good idea to me, wards are supposed to be in a straight line or circle."

Well, she had been patient for a while, at least.

"Wards don't have to be any shape, so long as they're continuous," Hugh said. "Drawing them in straight lines or circles is mostly just convention, along with being two of the most convenient shapes for wards."

"Mostly?" Godrick said nervously.

"There are cases where the shape matters more, but this isn't one of them," Hugh said.

Talia started to say something else, but Sabae hushed her. Talia stuck out her tongue at Sabae.

Hugh shook his head and went back to adding the additional spellforms to the ward. They'd essentially act as a bypass, redirecting the flow of mana away from the spellforms that would prevent Hugh and his friends from passing. The wards would still be operational, they just weren't worried about students passing through anymore. Of course, if the ward hadn't decayed, Hugh could never have gotten close enough to do this.

Very, very carefully, Hugh added one final connecting line, and… the chalk began to glow as the mana passed through it. It dimmed almost immediately, but Hugh could sense the mana was moving through it correctly.

"We're good to go! Be careful not to step on the chalk, that'll disrupt the bypass," Hugh said.

"It's really safe?" Godrick asked.

"Probably," Hugh said.

"Probably?" Godrick said.

"Probably," said Hugh, and opened the door.

CHAPTER TWELVE

The True Library

On the other side was… another storeroom, this one full of bookbinding supplies. Hugh shouldn't have been surprised- both sides of the door would really have to be out of the way in order for it to have been neglected. Hugh still felt his heart start beating faster as he stepped through the door, however.

Talia was so close on his heels that she almost pushed him through the door. Sabae followed soon after, with Godrick hesitantly taking the rear. Hugh pushed through the piles of bookbinding materials to the door out of the storeroom. Cautiously, he pushed it open, and then gasped in shock.

Hugh had expected the restricted section of the library to resemble the upper library. He was so, so very wrong.

The room they found themselves in was by far the largest room Hugh had ever seen in his life. The restricted section of the library was roughly cubical, and must have been at least four or five miles to a side. The room looked considerably bigger than the mountain Skyhold was built into. The walls were entirely lined with books, with a balcony winding completely around at around one story intervals. The balcony they were on was close to the top. If that had been all the books in the room, it would have been more books than Hugh had ever imagined even existed.

It wasn't even close to all the books in the room.

Immense stone bookshelves, hundreds of feet high, floated in neat, orderly rows in the huge space in the center of the room. Floating islands drifting near them had bookshelves, reading rooms, and in one case, what looked to be a thriving forest on top. Hugh spotted a couple of cubes with bookshelves on all the sides- including the bottom. There were a few paths leading out into the center room, stepping stones scattered here and there- but Hugh couldn't see a way to get to most of the floating structures.

Thousands upon thousands of origami golems were visible, tending to tasks all over the library. Books seemed to frequently decide to fly about on their own- some simply hovering through the air, others flapping their covers and pages like wings.

All of this was lit by a profusion of glowcrystals, floating wisps of light, and even a tiny sun orbiting the floating island with the trees on it, but the room was so huge the overall impression was one of general gloom and dimness.

Hugh silently walked forwards to the edge of the balcony. When he looked downwards, he couldn't even see the bottom of the library, except for a blue-white, unearthly glow coming from far below. The others silently stepped alongside him.

"How... how is this even possible?" Sabae said. "This is bigger than Skyhold. Bigger that the mountain Skyhold is built into. There can't be this many books in the entire world."

No one answered her. They all just stood there silently for ages. Hugh could see quite a few librarians, but the closest one had to be at least a half mile away.

"So much better than tha port," Godrick whispered finally.

Talia elbowed Hugh.

"What was that for?" Hugh said. "I swear, being friends with you is at least one third collecting new bruises."

"Look, an index node!" Talia said, not seeming to hear Hugh. Or choosing to ignore him.

The foursome strode over to the index node. The blank-paged volume was considerably larger than the index nodes in the upper library.

"What should we look up?" Sabae asked.

No one said anything for a moment, then Talia stepped up to the book. She picked up the quill beside it and simply wrote "dreamfire."

Nothing happened for a moment, and then in precise, bold letters, printed out a single sentence.

What about dreamfire?

Hugh stared silently at the book for a moment, then looked at Talia. She stared back at him. She slowly looked at the others, who just stared at her as well. She turned back to the book, and begin writing in it again.

What are some advanced dreamfire manifestation techniques?

What sort of techniques?

Combat techniques.

Nothing happened for a moment, then the words vanished off the page, it tore itself out of the book, and drifted up into the air. It revolved a few times, then began folding itself. Within seconds, a hummingbird origami golem fluttered in the air in front of them.

Talia slowly reached out to touch it, but the hummingbird shot away from her, coming to a halt twenty feet farther down the balcony. She turned to look at the rest of them, and then they all set out as one. Every time they approached the hummingbird it would dart off again to wait for them farther down. After about half a mile of walking, the hummingbird darted over to the shelf, where it hovered in front of a book with a fraying green cloth cover.

Talia reached out to the book. The instant her finger brushed it, the hummingbird darted off towards the nearest index node, where it unfolded itself and inserted itself into the book.

Talia pulled the book off the shelf. It looked like it would fall apart if anyone even looked at it for too long, but it was apparently much sturdier than it looked. The pages were lined with hard to read, handwritten text. Talia was slowly flipping through the book when the four noticed something. The letters were starting to glow with the purple-green light of dreamfire itself.

"Ah think ye should close tha book, Talia," Godrick said. Tiny tongues of dreamfire had actually begun to lick up from the letters at this point.

Talia slammed it shut. Hugh noticed that many of the threads that composed the cover were actually glowing, in patterns that looked suspiciously like spellforms.

No one said anything for a moment.

"How many of these books do you think also do stuff like that?" Sabae said.

"Quite ah few, ah'd guess," Godrick said. He shuffled nervously. "Ah reckon ah know why it's forbidden ta students."

A thought struck Hugh, and he strode over to the nearest index node. He picked up the quill on its stand, dipped it into the ink, and began to write.

How many books are in here?

The Index took a second to reply.

Unknown.

Then how do you keep track of all the books?

I only track the books that have been indexed.

How many books have been indexed?

Twelve million, four hundred thousand, seven hundred and sixty two.

As Hugh and the others watched, the sixty two became a sixty three, then a sixty four.

Where do all the books come from?

The Index paused for another moment.

Information restricted. Reason for query?

Hugh blinked, then quickly wrote again.

Just curious, it's not important.

The book didn't respond to that.

Hugh leaned back and looked at the others.

"Well, we know at least a few of them come from Alustin and the other librarian errants," Sabae said.

"Can ah try?" Godrick said.

Hugh passed him the quill.

Books on using scent attunements in battle. Preferably books that aren't booby trapped and are safe to handle.

How strong is said search preference?

Exceptionally strong.

The page tore itself out of the book, folded itself into a dragonfly, and shot off fifty feet down the shelves.

"I think we should split up and each meet back here in an hour," Hugh said. "There's more here than we could read in a lifetime."

Everyone nodded in agreement, eager to explore. Godrick headed off after the dragonfly.

Talia quickly stepped up to the book, and repeated her query on dreamfire- this time, however, making sure to include the bit about not being booby trapped. She then left in the same direction as Godrick, in pursuit of a tiny paper dragon.

Sabae stepped up next.

Do you have anything written by members of the Kaen Das family?

Yes. Fourteen private journals, three training manuals, a significant collection of personal correspondence, and an unknown volume that can only be opened by blood descendants of the Kaen Das family.

Sabae looked at Hugh in shock, then turned back to the book.

Take me to the unknown volume, please.

The page tore itself out of the book and folded itself into an origami fish, which promptly swam the opposite way from Godrick and Talia. Sabae turned to follow it.

Hugh stared at the index node for a time. What did he want to ask it? He was already overloaded with potential contract partners with Galvachren's Bestiary alone, so not for more potential options... Hmm.

Directions for completing a warlock pact.

Alustin had taught him a lot about warlockery, but he'd refused to share the spellforms to complete a warlock pact so far.

The page tore itself out of the book and folded itself into a tiny balloon, with a basket dangling below it. Hugh followed it for a time, until it abruptly made a left turn.

Off the edge of the balcony, into midair.

As it did so, a series of stepping stones flew from out of the depths of the room, forming a narrow footpath. The stepping stones floated independently, each about a short pace apart. Hugh gulped. He knelt down, reaching out to touch the first one. It felt absolutely stable, like it were embedded in an actual floor.

Then he reached around it and below it. There didn't appear to be anything holding it up.

Hugh stood up, and slowly rested his foot on the first stepping stone. He put more and more weight on it, but it never moved.

He pulled his foot back, turned around, and walked back to the nearest index node.

If I were to rip out pages before writing on them, could I write on them later and still get directions?

Yes, though it would only be necessary if you were going into a section of the library with few Index access nodes.

Hugh looked back out at the footpath.

He tore out four pages and tucked them into the back of his new spellbook, then latched it shut again. He carefully adjusted it to make sure it was secure over his shoulder, then walked back to the stepping stones.

Hugh took a deep breath, and carefully stepped out onto the path.

It was… a little easier than Hugh had expected. The stepping stones were decently large, and comfortably close together.

Unfortunately, Hugh still had to look down at his path to make sure he didn't fall, so he was staring down the miles tall drop the whole time. He crossed above several floating islands, wound between a massive pair of shelves filled with engraved clay tablets, and had to stop to let a flock of grimoires fly by. And the whole time, the drop loomed below him. Distantly below him he could see that blue-white glow. As he stared at it, he swore he could see something shifting and moving inside of it.

Abruptly, the path of stepping stones simply came to a halt against the side of a massive floating bookshelf. It must have extended two hundred feet above and below Hugh. At the end of the path the stepping stones had carefully organized themselves into a broad, level platform. Hugh gratefully stepped onto it, and eyed the origami balloon. It was floating in front of a rather bland, boring looking volume.

Hugh pulled it off the shelf.

The 74 Uses of Dragon Dung.

That… didn't seem quite right.

Hugh pulled the book off the shelf, but the balloon stayed right where it was. Behind where *The 74 Uses of Dragon Dung* had sat was a thin black volume. Hugh pulled it out, putting *The 74 Uses of Dragon Dung* back on the shelf. The instant he touched the black volume, the balloon flew away.

He opened the black volume to its first page.

In a well practiced, easily readable handwriting, the author had penned a short warning.

This volume is strictly forbidden from being read, except by those ranked at least Bishop or higher in the Church of The Eternal Heavenly Flame. In it are detailed some of the foulest, most pernicious pieces of magic ever devised. This volume only exists in order to offer ways to defeat these spells, in the off chance these heresies ever resurface and must be confronted again. Be warned, the spells grow progressively more deranged towards the end

121

of the book. The original scribe was driven quite insane by recording them, and ended up having to be committed to an asylum.

The warning was followed by a table of contents. The warlock pact spell was the third in the book, between something called Blisterpox Curse and a truth spell that apparently burned any lies spoken into the skin of the victim for the rest of their life.

Hugh wondered if it was significant that he'd never heard of the Church of the Eternal Heavenly Flame before.

He flipped to the warlock pact, expecting to see some hideously convoluted spellform.

It was fairly convoluted, but it was also surprisingly familiar. It was essentially structured similarly to a ward. It had places to write out the contract, as well as two blank spaces that the signers of the contract would touch at the same time to complete the ward and seal the pact. He did note that, indeed, the scribe who'd copied this spell down was different than the one who penned the warning.

Hugh pulled out his spellbook and quickly copied the warlock pact into it, along with all the relevant details. He made sure to hide the pact far towards the back of the book, so someone casually opening the book would be less likely to see it.

He probably wouldn't need the spell before this summer, when Alustin was supposed to take him to find a contract partner, but he wanted it just in case.

He finished copying the warlock pact down, and resisted the urge to peek farther back into the book. No sense in tempting fate. He tucked the slim volume back behind *The 74 Uses of Dragon Dung.*

Hugh pulled out one of the pages he'd pulled out of the index node, and requested a book on the principles of constructing large-scale wards, like the ones in Sabae's great grandmother's journal.

The journey wasn't nearly so bad this time- most of the route took him back along the path he'd followed before, merely branching off about halfway back, then returning. The book he found was a dry volume on mana loss rates and determining factors in ward efficiency. It didn't look entertaining, but it certainly looked useful.

He continued to keep his eyes down on the stepping stones the whole way back again, trying to keep down the vertigo. When he finally reached the balcony again, he grabbed the railing and took a deep breath. It felt really, really good to be standing on ground he couldn't see through.

Someone cleared their throat. Hugh looked up.

Talia, Sabae, and Godrick all stood looking uncomfortable in front of him. Between Hugh and his friends, however, stood Alustin, who raised his eyebrow at Hugh.

"Oops," said Hugh.

CHAPTER THIRTEEN

Punishment and Preparation

Alustin did not look amused.

"So whose idea was this little trip?" he said.

"Entirely mine," said Hugh immediately. "They only came along because it was my birthday, and I really wanted to do this."

Alustin arched his eyebrow.

"How interesting. I have four students all trying to take credit for the same plan."

Hugh opened his mouth, then shut it again.

Alustin sighed. "Well, at least no one can claim you aren't loyal to one another. I can, however, claim that you're all idiots for coming here in the first place. There is a very, very good reason why this room, the Grand Library, is forbidden to all but full mages. The Grand Library kills an average of two hundred people a decade, the vast majority of which are fully trained mages."

Talia mouthed "two hundred?" in shock.

"This part of the library is horrendously dangerous. It's the largest known collection of enchanted books in existence. Even many of the non-enchanted volumes are highly dangerous. Some contain information that can drive you mad, others are actually constructed of poisonous plants, for whatever insane reason."

Hugh thought guiltily of the book he'd found the warlock ritual in, but didn't say anything.

"How did you even get in here?" Alustin said.

No one said anything for a moment, then Hugh spoke up. "I reworked one of the wards."

Alustin stared at him for a second, then narrowed his eyes. "Don't lie to me, Hugh. How did you get in here? Did you steal a librarian's key?"

"I'm not lying!" Hugh said. "I really reworked one of the wards."

"He did," Godrick said defensively. "He's really good with wards."

Alustin stared at Hugh for an uncomfortably long amount of time. "Show me."

124

Hugh led Alustin to the storeroom door they had gotten in by. Alustin spent at least fifteen minutes staring at the ward, and at Hugh's notes. Finally, he looked up at Hugh.

"How long did you spend studying the ward?" Alustin said.

"Maybe thirty minutes?" Hugh said.

"Not even that," Sabae said.

Alustin sighed. "I'm torn between wanting to yell at you for messing with a ward that could have killed you and being impressed that you managed to bypass the ward at all."

"Kill me?" Hugh said. "Those spellforms should have just hurled me back, right?"

Alustin looked at him seriously. "At normal ward power levels, yes. We haven't particularly covered how wards are affected by the materials they're moving through to any great degree yet, however. Even as degraded as this ward is, however, with the power supplied by the library, you would have been mashed to a pulp."

Hugh felt a little sick.

Alustin sighed, then gestured them all out of the storeroom and back into the immense library room. "I'll send some librarians to take a look at this and restore the ward. And to safely remove your changes. In the meantime... Let's see what you all got."

Everyone looked blankly at Alustin.

"Your book selections, let's see them."

The four sheepishly handed over their books.

He spent a few moments browsing their selections. "Hugh, excellent choice, if a bit advanced. Let me know when you run across anything you don't understand in here- which will be often. That being said, what provoked you to look into large-scale wards? They're fiendishly difficult, and there's not a lot of demand outside some specialized applications."

Hugh told him about Sabae's great-grandmother's journal, and the family's potential job offer. Alustin actually looked impressed at that.

"I'd definitely like to take a look at that journal myself, if that's alright with you."

Hugh nodded, happy to talk about anything other than them trespassing.

"Onto the topic of Sabae... what on Earth possessed you to choose a book that can't be opened?"

"I can open it," Sabae said.

Sabae held out her hand. Alustin somewhat hesitantly handed the volume back. Hugh hadn't seen the book yet- the cover looked like glass or crystal, but with an actual storm bound inside. Hugh could even see the occasional bolt of lightning.

The instant Sabae touched the book, the storm drastically increased in intensity. Sabae opened it without a problem, and flipped through a few pages. Her hair appeared to be drifting in a faint breeze coming from the book, even after the pages stopped moving.

"This volume can only be opened by myself or another blood member of my family."

Alustin held out his hand. "May I take a look?"

Sabae appeared to think for a moment, then extended the open book. "Of course."

The instant Alustin reached for it, she snapped it shut and dropped it in his hand. "If, of course, you're a blood member of the Kaen Das family."

Alustin looked frustrated for a moment, then walked

with the book over to the nearest index node. He spent a few moments writing in the node, then tapped on the page three times with his knuckle, and the text erased itself.

"In that case, Sabae, as much as it pains me to give an enchanted grimoire of unknown contents away, I believe this is yours, and not the library's." Alustin reluctantly handed the grimoire back to Sabae, who tucked it under her arm, face composed.

Alustin turned to Godrick, examining his volume. As he did so, Hugh noticed a self satisfied grin briefly flash across Sabae's face. "Hmm. A perfectly reasonable choice, though I should note that the book is enchanted as well- it magnifies any scents it encounters, so be cautious with it, and don't bring it into any dining halls or restrooms."

Talia's book on dreamfire also passed muster. This one, thankfully, was not enchanted- Hugh doubted the first book on dreamfire would have passed.

"Well, at least I can't fault your choice of book selections," Alustin muttered. "So, punishments: You're all required to memorize everyone who has died or gone missing here in the Grand Library in the past decade, as well as their cause of death if it's known. It's been a relatively safe decade, we've only lost… one hundred and forty three, last time I checked."

Hugh looked out over the colossal room and gulped.

"Should… should we head somewhere else for this talk?"

Alustin grinned. "Now you're starting to respect the library properly. You should be fine so long as you stay with me and don't touch any books without asking me first. Still, though, it might be best if we do head out."

Alustin had turned to lead them out- not, Hugh

noticed, by the storeroom door they'd come in by, when Talia spoke up. "How can this place be so huge? It's bigger than the entire mountain Skyhold is built into!"

"That's because this room isn't precisely inside of the mountain."

"It's an extradimensional space?" Hugh said. He'd read about those- they increased the size of internal spaces, but were notoriously challenging enchantments to pull off, and they only increased available space a little bit.

Alustin stared off into space.

"In a sense, yes. The room started off that way, but the enchantment was only going to increase its internal size by a relatively small amount. Due to… unforeseen interactions with the magic of the labyrinth, however, it ended up much larger than expected, among other effects."

"What sort of interactions?" Hugh said.

"What was this space supposed to be originally?" Sabae said.

"What kinds a' other effects?" said Godrick.

Alustin gave them a cryptic look, then started walking.

"Let's get you all out of here."

Hugh had one more question. "What was that light down near the bottom?"

Alustin answered without looking back at him.

"It was the Great Index. Now let's go."

Alustin hadn't been joking about making them memorize everyone who had died in the Grand Library.

Anna Coldspark: *Fell to her death by not paying attention to the footpath she was supposed to be following.*
Unknown Mage #12: *Found half starved and dehydrated, as though they'd been wandering the Grand*

Library for years.

Helgrim the Corpulent: *Eaten by a flock of spellbooks.*

Durham the Grim: *Went missing without a trace. Two years later, a biography of him with covers of human bone and pages of human skin was found in the Library.*

Hugh grimaced and looked away from the list, then turned back to their other assignment.

Alustin and Artur Wallbreaker had decided that rather than spending the last two weeks before the labyrinth trying to teach the apprentices a few new spells, that they'd instead focus on three things: Practicing the skills they already had, learning more about the labyrinth, and, of course, memorizing the list of the victims of the Grand Library. Thankfully, they made the first two a much higher priority.

They still expected at least some memorization of the list by the apprentices in the meantime, unfortunately.

The reading about the labyrinth was much, much less disturbing than the reading about the Library. While the labyrinth was extremely dangerous, the uppermost level was considerably less so. Some students died during this test, but it was pretty rare- and, of those, the overwhelming majority died by being foolish and going to a lower level. Still, deaths had been known to happen on the first floor, which is why students were required to travel in teams.

Unfortunately, they wouldn't be able to plot out a route through the labyrinth beforehand. Like the more dangerous lower levels, the top level of the labyrinth was apparently capable of altering its shape. No one had ever seen it happen, but they'd seen the results.

Still, there tended to be a few common themes. The

first level was roughly circular, with multiple entrances on the outside. In the center was a large, circular room with a stairwell leading downwards to the next level. It was the main exit to the lower levels, though other stairwells down were known to occur.

In that center room would be waiting a team of full mages, who were there for three purposes- to hand out tokens to students who made it to them proving they'd been to the center, to prevent students from going farther down, and to prevent especially dangerous monsters from moving upwards onto the first floor. The students merely had to reach the center room, retrieve a token apiece from the mages, then make it back to any exit.

Of course, it wasn't that simple. Apart from being a fiendishly difficult maze, even the first floor of the labyrinth had plenty of traps and monsters. Nothing a decently trained apprentice mage couldn't handle, generally, but plenty of students failed every year.

So Hugh and the others spent hours every day reading past accounts of the first floor, guides to the various creatures and traps found there, and planning out their strategy.

The time spent mastering their abilities was where things really got brutal. Before, Alustin and Artur had merely demanded competence when teaching. Now, however, they were demanding perfection, and it was exhausting. Sabae was expected to be able to release a gust strike on demand, and she was expected to be able to manifest wind armor over her shins and calves for minutes at a time as well. Talia's targeting with her dreamfire bolts was expected to be perfect.

And Hugh? Hugh was expected to be able to cast all of his basic cantrips perfectly, without any delay. This…

really wasn't that much of a challenge at this point, but that didn't relieve Hugh that much. Simply speaking, without a warlock pact, Hugh's lack of attunements made him by far the weakest member of the team. Hugh's large mana reservoirs meant he never really ran out of mana casting cantrips, but there definitely was a hard upper limit on the power of cantrips.

His special project should help a little bit, but Hugh was still extremely worried about holding his friends back. Not just in that their team would have one less effective combatant, but that they'd have to spend time actively protecting him.

When he confronted Alustin about it, Alustin merely told him that "he just needed to trust in himself and in his friends."

Hugh did trust his friends. He just didn't trust himself.

CHAPTER FOURTEEN

Entering the Labyrinth

Hugh stared at the massive stone doors to the labyrinth. They were crystalline and opaque, rather than granite like the rest of the mountain. Hugh couldn't make out any details, but they were covered in absurdly intricate spellform engravings. He hadn't the slightest idea of what they did.

"Tha doors are made a' quartzite," Godrick said nervously. The huge youth looked as nervous as Hugh felt, toying with the massive steel sledgehammer he'd be

131

bringing with him into the labyrinth. "It's basically sandstone that's been crushed and heated over millenia. Much stronger, but much harder to manipulate with mana."

"It just looks like a big lump of dirty crystal to me," Talia snapped. She fingered the two daggers on her belt irritably. She'd been even more impatient and standoffish the closer the test got, and now that it was here, she looked like she was ready to explode at the slightest provocation. Hugh had noticed, however, that her foot hadn't stopped nervously tapping since they'd arrived at this labyrinth entrance.

"Crystals are just shinier rocks, aren't they?" Sabae asked. She looked almost as cool and collected as usual, but her shoulders were just a little bit stiffer, her movements just a little bit jerkier, and her normally calm voice sounded just a little bit forced.

Godrick opened his mouth to respond when a mage strode through the crowd of students to the door. Hugh didn't recognize her, but that wasn't surprising- there were thousands of full mages in Skyhold, and not all of them could be as well known as Aedan Dragonslayer, Sulassa Tidecaller, or Artur Wallbreaker.

"Apprentices, if I could have your attention," the middle-aged woman called. It took a moment, but eventually everyone quieted down. Amusingly, the instructors who had come to watch their students set off were among the last to quiet down. Hugh looked back to see Alustin looking straight at him. Alustin nodded, and Hugh took a deep breath and looked back at the mage in front of the doors.

"In just a few short moments I'll be opening these doors for you to enter. You will enter in three minute intervals by team in the order announced. We will be sending the teams judged most capable first, since there will be a higher risk of earlier teams encountering monsters and other threats. The other five doors to the first level of the labyrinth will be opening at the same time. In order to pass this class, you'll need to make it to the center of the first level of the labyrinth…"

Hugh couldn't help but tune out the mage a little as she repeated the rules and warnings they'd all heard a dozen times before. He rocked back and forth on the balls of his feet and stared at the massive, crystalline doors nervously. He was sure that his team would be very far down the list. Even with a magical powerhouse like Godrick on their team, the reputations of the others as useless in one way or another would surely drag them down the list. Hugh especially. Alustin might be changing things for them, but they'd have to prove themselves to have anyone believe otherwise.

The one thing Hugh was really happy about? Rhodes and his team were entering from a different door.

"…and, under no circumstances are you to take any stairway down or other downward path. Even if you see another student lying injured at the base of a short ramp heading downwards, you are not to help them. Instead, take note of the location and let the first instructor you see know."

There was silence for a moment as the mage unraveled a scroll.

"First team: Godrick son of Artur Wallbreaker. Sabae Kaen Das. Talia of Clan Castis. Hugh of Emblin."

Hugh overbalanced and fell in surprise.

Godrick caught Hugh before he fell very far and set

him back on his feet. Hugh gulped nervously and looked around.

Everyone was staring at them. He could see them whispering among themselves, and even overheard someone say "Emblin." He felt his face turn red.

"If you'd start a line by the door, please," the mage with the scroll said.

Hugh gulped.

Sabae was the first to move, and the other two quickly followed her. Hugh took a second longer, then hurried to catch up to them. He could feel everyone still staring.

"Tannis Rootborn, Elia Karnath…" Hugh glanced back at the second team. They all looked incredibly intimidating. One had an arm that appeared to be made of a living treebranch, inscribed with intricate spellforms. Another was hairless, and had what looked to be glowing wires embedded in her otherwise bald scalp. The third looked to be partially covered in frost, and the final one had what looked like scarabs climbing all over them.

"Why aren't they going first?" Hugh whispered to Sabae as they came to a halt in front of the doors. "They look absolutely terrifying!"

Sabae glanced back at the second group, then back at Hugh.

"Hugh, I don't know if you've noticed, but we look somewhat terrifying ourselves. Godrick's the size of a house and has a hammer most people couldn't lift; Talia is almost entirely covered in spellform tattoos, looks like she wants to bite someone's throat out all the time, and has a reputation for destroying classrooms; and I'm covered in scars and from one of the most respected mage families on the continent."

Hugh blinked. When she put it like that he supposed

his friends were fairly intimidating. But… "I'm not, though. I'm just a skinny little country bumpkin."

Sabae frowned at him. "Look at the teams that are lining up right now."

Hugh looked back. Several other teams had lined up already, and they all looked almost as intimidating as the team just behind them. Especially a short figure in a cloak whose shadow kept moving on its own.

"They're all terrifying," Hugh said.

"They're all visibly terrifying," Sabae said. "You're in the first group, and you look… utterly normal. No weird tattoos, no bonded magical weapons passed down through your family, no familiar. No costume to try and make yourself look more dangerous, either. Their imaginations must be running wild trying to figure out what kind of mage you are."

Hugh was taken aback at this. He looked back at the other apprentices in line again, and realized something.

They were all more terrified than terrifying. The student with the treebranch arm couldn't stop nervously tracing the contours of his arm. The shadow of the figure in the cloak wasn't being aggressive, but was twitching nervously.

"They're all as nervous as we are, Hugh. Most of them probably count themselves as lucky they're not going first."

Hugh took a deep breath and nodded. Sabae was probably right about that. And the other students were definitely correct to count themselves as lucky.

It was at that point that the librarian paused in reading her list. "We'll finish lining you up in a moment, but it appears to be time to send in the first team."

Hugh felt his heart rate pick up even more.

135

The mage strode over to the doors and rested her hand on a particular spellform pattern. It began to glow with a warm, pulsing light. She then strode over to the matching pattern on the other door and did the same. The instant she took her hand off of the door, light began to travel outwards from the glowing patterns along the lines of the spellforms. Within instants, the crystalline doors were covered in glowing lines that intersected, split, merged, and formed eye-twisting geometrical patterns. Then, the light seemed to sink downwards into the crystal.

Then the doors simply went dark.

For a single moment, Hugh felt relief at the thought that something had gone wrong, and that they wouldn't have to take the test after all.

Then the massive doors silently and slowly opened inwards onto darkness.

Hugh and the other apprentices stared into the darkness of the labyrinth. None of them made any move to step forwards.

"Well?" prompted the mage who had just opened the doors.

Hugh gulped and looked at the others. Then, as one, they stepped forwards toward the doors. Hugh compulsively checked his equipment as he strode forwards. Dagger from Talia on his belt, check. Spellbook over his shoulder, check. Waterskin, check. Secret project... check.

As they strode across the threshold of the labyrinth, the temperature dropped abruptly. Not to the point where extra clothes were needed, but enough to where Hugh felt a little uncomfortable.

The walls of the labyrinth were back to the normal

granite of Skyhold, but they were intricately covered in spellform designs that made even the ones on the door look simple. They covered every inch of the walls, floor, and ceiling.

The room of the labyrinth that they'd entered was a half-moon in shape, with the door out on the flat wall. It was lit solely by the light coming through the door. There were three hallways branching off from the curved wall, each quickly fading into darkness.

"Which way should we go?" said Hugh. He crafted a basic light cantrip in his mind's eye, then summoned it in his hand.

"If this were a normal maze," Sabae said, "we should just pick a direction and take it whenever we came to a turn, but that's not an especially effective strategy in this labyrinth."

They all stood silently for a moment, and then Talia nodded to herself. "Doesn't really matter which way we go, then. We just need to figure out the curve of the circle and head inwards."

Talia strode towards the hallway on the right. No one else moved for a second, then everyone else rushed to catch up with her. Godrick summoned a light from his hand as well.

"Ah'm supposed ta be in front with Sabae, remember?" Godrick said.

Talia snorted, but let Godrick and Sabae pull in front of them. Their team had not one, but two close-range combat mages, so it made sense to put them where they would be the first to run into any threats. Most teams didn't have any, so their team might actually have an edge in case of ambushes.

They all stayed quiet as they strode down the hallway.

It curved gradually, and soon the only light visible came from Hugh and Godrick's cantrips, and the only noise came from their footsteps.

"I wish we could have used yarn or chalk to mark our path," Hugh finally muttered to himself. He almost jumped at how loud it sounded in the quiet of the hallway. The others all looked at him, and he blushed. "I know why we can't, I'm just saying." The enchantments of the labyrinth seemed to have been built with the intention of, among other things, preventing people from cheating while navigating the maze. Strings would be cut, chalk would wash away, and so on and so forth.

No one spoke for another minute or so, until they came to the first fork in the path. The right-hand path continued along the same curve they were walking, but the left-hand path seemed to head inwards.

"Like Talia said, we do need to head inwards," Sabae said.

They cautiously started down the left-hand path. They were only a few hundred feet down it when Talia hissed and came to a halt.

"What is it?" Hugh said.

"Shh," hissed Talia.

Everyone remained silent. After a few seconds, Hugh heard it too- some sort of chittering, scuttling noise. He couldn't tell which direction it was coming from, though.

"Behind us!" said Talia.

Hugh whirled around, aiming his light cantrip behind them, but didn't see anything. Godrick and Sabae moved forwards in front of Hugh, and Talia stepped beside him. Godrick readied his hammer, while whirlwinds had begun to spin around Sabae's forearms and calves. Dreamfire was rising out of Talia's palms. Hugh pulled his secret project out of his belt pouch.

"Somethin' smells awful," Godrick said. Hugh sniffed, but didn't smell anything yet. It must be Godrick's scent affinity helping him smell things farther away.

Something came skittering out of the darkness on all fours and stopped, hissing at them.

It was about the size of a cat, with a batlike face and a fleshy, humanoid body and a protuberant gut. Clumps of hair stuck out of it almost at random, and Godrick was right- it stank horribly.

"It's an imp!" Hugh said.

"A what?" said Talia?

"A lesser demonspawn. About as smart as a rat, and much more vicious. They also…"

Almost a dozen more came into the light and began hissing. Hugh could hear more in the shadows, and see some of their eyes glinting in the dark.

"Run in packs," Hugh finished weakly.

The first imp launched itself into the air at Godrick. Before it could get close, Talia sent it flying with a blast of dreamfire. It crashed to the ground, melting into a pile of goo.

As if that were a signal, the other imps began launching themselves at the foursome. Godrick yelled and smashed his sledgehammer down, pulping two of them. Sabae kicked one, releasing a gust of wind that sent a whole crowd of them flying backwards. Talia launched dreamfire bolt after dreamfire bolt into the crowd, each of which exploded, crushed, froze, or aged an imp into oblivion.

"Hugh, do something!" Talia yelled.

Hugh shook off the fear that had gripped him and readied his secret project.

It was a sling. An ordinary sling, just like the one he'd used back in the woods of Emblin to hunt rabbits and pheasants. He'd crafted this one out of leather he'd found in a bookbinding supply store-room. It was well made, but nothing special. The ammunition, however...

The ammunition was special. He'd spent hours on every single little sphere of rock, painstakingly carving wards into them. He only had a dozen of them, so they'd better work.

Hugh spun up the sling, wardstone in the cup, and released it straight at the floor in the crowd of imps. The instant the wardstone struck the stone floor, the spellform was broken, and all the energy stored up inside the ward was released.

And there was a lot of energy stored in it. At least a half dozen imps were caught in the blast. They weren't just killed- they were pulped. A shower of liquefied imp splattered over the four of them, smelling even worse than when they were alive.

Talia wiped imp gore from her face and glared at Hugh. "Well, don't quit now!" She hurled another dreamfire bolt at an imp. This one, surprisingly, actually just burned.

Hugh quickly began spinning up his sling again, as Godrick impaled another imp with a spike of stone he summoned from the floor and Sabae sent a gust of wind scything across the floor with a kick, tumbling imps wildly.

The fight against the imps seemed to go on for hours, though it was probably only minutes. By the time they were done, they were drenched in bits of imp, and a solitary straggler scuttled off into the darkness the way it had came.

"Well, that's these clothes ruined," Talia said.

Everyone stared at her for a moment, then burst out laughing.

Once the hysterical laughter had stopped, Hugh began casting a new cantrip. This was one of his favorites- a cleaning cantrip. He used it to suction off the imp goo off of all of them.

"You might be my favorite person right now," Sabae said.

Talia sniffed herself.

"We still smell awful," she said. "Godrick, think you can do some scent magic?"

Godrick shuffled his feet a bit. "Ah'm not tah great with scent magic yet. Ah'd probably make things worse."

"I've got that one covered too- with a little help from Godrick," Hugh said. He rummaged through his belt pouch, finally pulling out a little glass sphere- the scent removing sphere Godrick had given him for his birthday.

"Now this is why we're the team that was sent in first," Sabae said, grinning.

They were attacked twice more by imps on their way towards the center. They won through both times, though Godrick got a nasty bite on one leg and Sabae's hands were repeatedly clawed up. Each time, Hugh happily cleaned up afterwards. They were also attacked by some sort of turtle spider that was nearly six feet across, but it was relatively slow moving, so Talia just pelted it with dreamfire as they retreated until the thing died silently.

They didn't find many traps, surprisingly. Tripwires, dart traps (usually unpoisoned), and non-fatal pitfalls were supposed to be common on this level, but they only found a single dart trap (which hit Godrick right in the backside, much to the others' amusement, especially Talia's) and a coughing gas trap.

The maze itself made a much more formidable challenge. They hit dead ends six times, found themselves going in circles twice, and frequently heard monsters or other students around a corner, only to turn it and find nothing. Hugh was sure that they were getting steadily closer to the center.

They reached the center of the first floor about two hours into the test. The center was a huge round room about two hundred feet across, with a large spiral staircase descending into the floor in the center. A good half-dozen mages maintained a magical dome-shaped barrier over it. The spellforms covering the walls, floor, and ceiling all seemed to lead out of the hole the staircase descended into. Or maybe into it.

They weren't the first team to arrive- despite being one of the first teams in, they were the eleventh team to get to the center. One other team was there when they arrived, and they mentioned encountering far, far more traps, including a snake trap, but no monsters. Hugh glanced at his bag of wardstone projectiles- he only had four left.

The mages in the center room handed out tokens to all four of them. "Remember," one of them said, "you can only pass the test if you return out the exit with a token. If you lose yours, you'll need to return here."

"Can other teams try to steal our tokens?" Talia asked.

"They can, but it won't count as a win for them- the tokens only work for the apprentice we hand them to. You'll still have to return here, though."

The mage shook all of their hands and wished them luck.

"Does anyone have any preference for which path we

should take out of the center?" Sabae asked.

"Let's just go back the way we came," Talia said, and started to head back that way. Sabae grabbed her by the shoulder and stopped her.

"Odds are that won't work- the labyrinth seems to dislike backtracking. Trying to do it usually leads you farther away."

Talia shrugged. "You all paid a lot more attention to the books on it than I did."

Hugh gestured towards one of the hallways leading outwards. "Let's take that one."

"It looks like all a' tha others," Godrick said.

"My gut is giving me a good feeling about it," Hugh said.

No one had any better ideas, so they headed down that direction.

About ten minutes after leaving the center, Hugh heard a click and froze.

"Did anyone else hear that?" he asked.

"Hugh, don't move," Talia said. "If you move, it'll activate."

Hugh looked down. The spellform he'd stepped on had sunk slightly into the ground and was glowing. Hugh could hear a rumbling sound in the distance.

"That's not how spellform traps work!" Hugh yelled. "Everyone run!"

He followed his own advice and took off forwards in a dead sprint.

Everyone else followed him, and just in time, too- a massive, spherical boulder dropped out of the ceiling above the spot where they had been standing. Everyone came to a halt, staring at it. It hadn't started rolling after them, thankfully.

"I thought you had a good feeling about this path, Hugh?" Talia asked.

"I did," Hugh said. "We're all okay, so I wasn't wrong."

Spellforms began to light up on the spherical boulder.

"Nevermind, I was wrong, everyone run!"

The boulder started rolling after them. Purposefully.

"I'm never trusting your gut again, Hugh!" Talia said. They all started running again.

The boulder chased them for a solid ten minutes before its spellforms dimmed and it gave up the chase. It had followed them relentlessly until then, even turning to follow them down the various forks they'd taken. Well, probably followed Hugh, since he triggered the trap, but the others weren't likely to abandon him.

If it hadn't been for the physical training that Alustin had demanded of them, Hugh doubted they could have kept ahead of it.

The square chamber they found themselves in had three exits- the one they'd come in from and two others placed on the adjacent sides of the room. The final wall was blank. They stayed there for several minutes catching their breath before Talia spoke up.

"Hugh, which way is your gut telling us to go? Because my gut's telling me we should go the opposite way from that."

Hugh ignored her, staring at the blank wall without an exit. He narrowed his eyes staring at it, then opened his sketchbook.

"Something's weird about that wall," he said.

He quickly began sketching the spellforms on the wall, identifying the important ones.

"Shouldn't we get moving?" Sabae said.

"Hold on just a minute longer," Hugh said.

Hugh grinned, looking back and forth between the wall and his drawings. "Hah! There's a secret door hidden here!"

"Really?" Godrick asked excitedly. "Will there be treasure behind it? Me da found his enchanted hammer in the depths of the labyrinth."

Hugh pulled out his chalk. "Let's find out."

It took another ten minutes before he was done altering the spellforms with chalk. The secret door was held shut by a spellform that was incredibly close to a ward in function. It was supposed to be opened by knowing... the answer to some sort of riddle, it looked like, but Hugh was able to bypass it.

When he drew the last chalk mark, the ward and the chalk marks drawn on it all lit up. The circular segment of wall in the middle seemed to just... dissolve away.

Hugh passed through the entrance first, not bothering to wait for Sabae or Godrick to go first. He was a little consumed by dreams of treasure, to say the least. He'd strode about halfway into the room when someone came in a doorway on the other side.

Rhodes.

Rhodes and Hugh froze, staring at each other in surprise, as their respective teams filtered into the room after them.

Rhodes armed for battle looked much more intimidating than usual. He wore a fine chainmail shirt, some sort of magical headband covered in glowing jewels and spellforms, and had a spear with a long metal head hovering in the air next to him. It didn't appear to have any spellforms attached to it, so Hugh guessed Rhodes

145

was holding it up with his attunement- or at least one of them.

The blue haired twins were with him as well, as was another boy who had lines of purple, glowing energy running up his arms. The twins were casting light generating cantrips.

No one spoke for a minute until Rhodes broke the silence.

"Well, well, well, look what we have here. A worthless sheepherder, his two whores, and a dumb brute."

Hugh flushed red. Talia stepped forwards, growling audibly, but Sabae spoke up first.

"Really? That's the best set of insults you can come up with? I'm going to have to give it a... solid D grade."

Hugh blinked at her.

"The sheepherder bit you've used often enough, and it clearly gets to Hugh, but calling us whores? That's just lazy. And calling Godrick a dumb brute? You should see his homework sometime, we go to him for help more often than not."

Rhodes blinked in confusion. Sabae was smiling cruelly at Rhodes.

"No offense to either Hugh or Talia, but angering them isn't exactly hard," Sabae said.

"Especially not Talia," Godrick muttered. Talia kicked him in the shin.

"So, if you'll excuse us, we'll be going now. We've got a test to finish." Sabae turned to leave.

"You're not going anywhere unless I say you can!" Rhodes snapped.

"Really?" Sabae said.

"Yes, really!" Rhodes snapped.

"No, I was asking if your banter could get any more

boring and unoriginal. You really have depended on your position more than your wit, haven't you?"

Hugh's mouth was hanging open in shock as he stared at Sabae. He felt a grin slowly creep across his face.

"What do your cronies think? You there, with the blue hair, are you actually that impressed with Rhodes' insults?"

The twins, not sure who she was referring to, looked at each other in confusion. Rhodes, standing in front of them, didn't see that, and seemed to assume that they were being silent because they couldn't make themselves praise his insults. He turned bright red.

"You can't..." he started, then Sabae interrupted.

"Where you about to tell me that I can't talk to you like that? Which, normally, would be followed by me telling you that I just had, and then you'd demand by what right I dared do so, and so on and so forth. Let's just skip all that, shall we? We have better things to do."

Talia started laughing. Rhodes' glare snapped to her.

"You damn..."

"Where you about to call her a barbarian, Rhodes?" Hugh said. "Or maybe a ginger bitch? Sabae's right, you're really pretty predictable."

Hugh felt shocked at his own courage. He might be no match for Rhodes, but... he'd always faced Rhodes feeling like he was alone before, like he had no one to back him up.

This time, he'd be damned if he was going to let that rich asshole walk all over him.

Hugh had never seen Rhodes this angry before. The female twin reached her hand out to Rhodes.

"Let's go, they're not worth it."

Rhodes shrugged off her hand and snarled.

147

"You… you… you worthless…" Rhodes looked like his head was about to explode.

Rhodes' spear hurling itself through the air at them clued Hugh into the fact that maybe they had pushed things a little too far.

The spear crossed the room in the blink of an eye, but came to a dead halt inches in front of Hugh's face. Rhodes bellowed, but the spear didn't move even a fraction of an inch closer.

Hugh looked behind him to see Godrick's face straining with effort. He'd managed to use his steel affinity to catch the spear just in time. Godrick's face screwed up even tighter with effort, and Hugh was afraid for a moment that he would lose the battle of wills.

Instead, the spear crept backwards an inch.

Slowly but surely the spear crept backwards across the room. About halfway across, it flipped over, the point facing towards Rhodes.

Things happened very, very quickly all of a sudden. Rhodes ducked and surrendered control of the spear to Godrick, and it clattered against the wall behind him. At almost the same moment, Rhodes released a bolt of lightning straight towards them. Hugh was convinced he was about to be fried like an insect.

Sabae caught it.

Everyone stared at her for a moment in shock as she clutched the writhing lightning between her fingers. Hugh could see burns forming on her hands. Then, with a jerk, she hurled it away from herself, right at the floor between them.

At which point Hugh noticed something he really really should have noticed before.

There weren't any spellforms on the floor in this room.

The lightning hit, and the floor shattered apart.
Hugh fell.

CHAPTER FIFTEEN

The Deeps

Hugh barely thought as he fell, and just started crafting a spell as fast as he could in his mind's eye. He used the most powerful spellform foundation he knew. He added his definitive and aiming lines quickly, then added a series of modifying lines that would let him start the power off low and quickly grow higher, rather than going full power off at once.

While he was doing this, he was trying to correct his tumble so he could focus on the ground. He managed to slow his fall enough to focus his cantrip light on the ground, and then frantically activated the spell.

Hugh could feel the mana flooding out of his reservoirs like nothing he'd ever felt before, and then he felt himself slowing. He came to a near complete halt, then his feet gently touched down on the ground. He frantically looked around him, and sighed as he saw his friends touch down on the ground next to him just as softly. The spell had worked. Hugh felt utterly drained magically. Stopping four people from falling to their deaths was far, far beyond the power levels cantrips were meant to channel.

No, six people. Rhodes and the male twin were down here too.

Hugh readied himself to continue the fight when he saw Sabae crumple. Godrick managed to catch her before she hit the ground.

"I'm okay," Sabae said. "Just… that took it out of me."

"Yeh caught lightning! That's amazing!" Godrick said.

Talia advanced towards Rhodes. "She caught *his* lightning. What the hell is wrong with you, Charax?"

Rhodes was looking around frantically. "We're below the first level! We shouldn't be here. We really shouldn't be here."

Hugh blinked, then looked around. They were in a roughly cylindrical room leading upwards. He glanced up the shaft, seeing a light far above where the other two members of Rhodes' team waited above. Then, something glinting plummeted down.

Rhodes' spear.

Hugh frantically reached into his pouch for his sling and a wardstone, but Rhodes didn't have any interest in fighting them. He caught the spear in his hand, and the twin grabbed the shaft as well. With a burst of wind that pushed Hugh backwards a few steps, Rhodes launched himself and his teammate into the air, rapidly moving up the shaft.

"A real courageous dragonslayer in the making, that one," Talia said dryly.

"So he's got a wind attunement too," Hugh said, "on top of his lightning and steel attunements."

"'e doesn't 'ave a steel attunement," Godrick said. "'e's got a wood attunement. He was pushing on tha shaft of tha spear, not tha head. That's why ah could overpower him."

"He was right, though," Sabae said. "We really shouldn't be here."

Up above, the light from Rhodes' teams light cantrips had vanished.

"If we wait here, maybe they'll alert an instructor like

they're supposed to?" Hugh said.

Talia looked at him and snorted.

Hugh sighed. "Right, can't count on that."

"You're right to be worried," a voice from the shadows said. Hugh whirled to face one of the entrances into the room. As he did so, a huge shape unfolded itself out of the pitch black hallway. And kept unfolding itself. And kept unfolding itself. "You seem quite wonderfully resourceful for your age. Most students would have died from that fall, but not you, young warlock. Still, these depths are far, far too dangerous for apprentices."

The figure, a full fifteen feet in height now, stepped into the light.

Hugh gasped, and he heard equally frightened reactions from the others.

It was a demon.

The demon was surprisingly similar to the imps they'd come across on the first floor. It had a batlike face, hairy protrusions all over its body, and arms that were disproportionately long, ending in razor sharp claws. In addition, however, it also had a long, hairless, prehensile tail ending in a stinger. Some sort of black ichor dripped out of the tip of it, sizzling when it hit the ground. The demon's most notable feature, however, was its gut. It protruded outward grotesquely, with transparent skin showing its intestines. They resembled nothing so much as a squirming mass of tadpoles.

"No need to be afraid, Hugh. I intend you no harm." The demon smiled in what it probably intended to be a reassuring manner, but the mouthful of fangs it revealed did quite the opposite.

"How do you know my name?" Hugh demanded.

"I watch the academy above me quite closely, Hugh," the demon said. "You may call me Bakori. It's merely a fragment of my name, but the rest would be... difficult for you to pronounce."

Hugh took a step back towards the others. "What do you want?"

"I want to help you. I bear no ill will towards the academy or its residents, despite their... antipathy towards my kind. Oh, and while we're at it, I should apologize for the behavior of my spawn. Imps aren't... the most polite or intelligent of beings."

"Help him how?" Talia demanded suspiciously.

Bakori glanced at her, then back at Hugh. "By offering him the power he needs to save his friends."

A suspicion grew in the back of Hugh's head. "You want me to sign a warlock pact with you."

"To put it simply, yes. These levels are extremely dangerous, and it's improbable that you'll make it back to the surface alive. I know how important your friends are to you, Hugh, and I'm quite willing to help you save them." Bakori smiled again.

"And what if I decline? You eat us?" Hugh said.

Bakori gave Hugh a hurt expression. "I'm offended that you'd think so low of me. Just more examples of the hate your kind holds for mine. No, if you refuse, I'll simply allow you to go your own way."

Hugh opened his mouth to reject Bakori's offer out of hand, and then paused. Bakori... wasn't wrong about their chances. Alustin and the other instructors had repeatedly drilled their warnings about the lower levels to the apprentices, noting how many students who even ended up on the second floor died. This... seemed like it was well below the second floor.

"What floor are we on?" Hugh asked, stalling for time.

"The sixth," Bakori said.

Hugh stood thinking as Bakori waited patiently. The sixth level was even deeper than Hugh had expected. Most adventurers visiting Skyhold seldom made it this far without extensive preparations. What chance did he and his friends have to escape on their own?

"Well, young warlock? What will it be?"

Hugh opened his mouth to answer, terrified that it was going to be the wrong choice, when Talia spoke up again. "He won't do it."

Sabae spoke up right on Talia's heels. "Hugh's too good of a person to make a deal with a demon."

Godrick spoke up next. "We'll find a way ta get back ta the surface on our own somehow."

Bakori looked at the three. For a brief instant, irritation swept across his face, then he turned back to Hugh.

"Do they speak for you, young warlock?"

Hugh couldn't find his voice at first. He hoped he was making the right decision here. He swallowed, then spoke up. "They do."

Bakori stared at him expressionlessly. "Very well. I'll leave the four of you to it." He turned to leave, then paused. "Though, if you change your mind, Hugh, you must only call my name three times in a row and will me to your side, and I will come to you, no matter the danger you are in. I offer not just power, but friendship as well."

With that, Bakori crouched to fit back into the tunnel and was gone.

"So what do we do now?" Sabae asked. She was standing on her own again, somewhat recovered from catching Rhodes' lightning bolt.

"We find our way back up," Talia said, not taking her eyes off of the exit Bakori had taken.

"How are we supposed to do that?" Hugh said.

"We stick together," Godrick said, "and we keep our heads clear."

"We should head out now, before that demon changes his mind about eating us," Talia said.

"He's not going to eat us," Hugh said.

"How do you know?" said Talia.

"Because he wants me to sign that contract with him. He wants something from me, and he's not going to rest until he gets it."

Everyone was silent for a time.

"Is there any way for us to get back up this way?" Sabae asked.

Godrick walked over to the wall. "Ah could try reshaping tha stone inta a ladder."

He reached out towards the stone. There was a flash, and he pulled his hand back, cursing. "Damn stone burnt me!"

Hugh walked over to look at the spellforms on the wall. They were very, very different than any spellforms he'd seen in the labyrinth so far- they were constructed to carry a truly massive amount of mana through their lines. It was all directional, as well- the mana was only moving upwards.

"I think this is some kind of mana conduit," Hugh said. "I've been wondering about whether the labyrinth absorbs or releases mana- it seems like the latter."

"Maybe we should focus less on trying to learn, more on trying to get out of here?" Talia said. "Is it safe for Godrick to reshape or not?"

"Definitely not," Hugh said. "Any more changes than

he tried to make probably would have overloaded him with mana and incinerated him."

Godrick paled at that.

"Well, can you… turn off the mana conduit?" Sabae said.

Hugh shook his head vigorously. "That's way, way past my skill level."

"We should get a move on, then," Talia said.

The others nodded in agreement.

Hugh gave the exit Bakori had taken one final look, before turning to follow his friends.

The sixth level of the labyrinth was similar to the first in a few ways- the tunnels were the same size, and the spellforms still covered nearly every surface. There were plenty of differences, though. The tunnels were more rounded than square, but the biggest difference was the noise.

Where the first floor was almost deathly quiet, the sixth floor… never was. There was wind down here, for some reason, and it was never silent. Worse, the wind carried other noises on it- chittering, footsteps, growls, and grinding mechanical noises. The four of them clustered closely together as they moved slowly down the hallways of the labyrinth. No one spoke. A few times Hugh thought he saw something moving at the edge of the light their cantrips provided, but it always vanished when he looked closer.

None of them had any idea what the layout of this level was like- they'd only seriously studied the first level. Students were never sent this deep. Just to be cautious, they moved extremely slowly, though they had to fight their desire to get out of there as quickly as possible.

Running across a trap this deep could be fatal.

They'd been moving through the branching corridors for about an hour when they came across something different.

The room they had stumbled into was nearly the size of the Great Hall where the Choosing had taken place. The ceiling wasn't as high as the Great Hall's, but it was still several times the height of the hallways.

And, best of all, there was a tunnel leading out of the upper story of the room.

The other notable feature of the room was the stone statues. They were everywhere- statues of knights, gargoyles, bulls, and more. Instead of the tough granite the walls were made of, the statues were carved out of marble.

Hugh pointed at the tunnels up above. "I'd bet that that tunnel is part of the fifth level, not the sixth."

Talia cursed. "How are we supposed to get up there? Stack up the statues?"

Godrick waled over to the wall. "Ah could try ta reshape a ladder out a' tha stone, but it would take a while."

Hugh checked the spellforms on the walls. "It doesn't look like these walls will react like the ones before, it should be safe for you to reshape the stone."

"I'd rather wait here and have a sure way up than wander more and potentially run into monsters," Sabae said.

Godrick nodded and walked over to the wall. He reached his hands out, and the stone started to slowly reshape itself like putty in his hands.

Unfortunately, that wasn't the only stone that started moving. The statues nearby started creaking and moving, jerkily moving their heads towards the apprentices.

"Goatshit in a picnic basket," Talia said.

"Should we run?" Hugh asked.

Godrick strode up beside them, sledgehammer at the ready, as the statues slowly closed in on them. "We can still fight our way out a' here, if we need to," he said.

Sabae shook her head. "We might not get a better chance to move up to the next level. Get back to the ladder, we'll hold them off for as long as you need."

Sabae clenched her fists, walked up to the nearest statue, an armored knight, and unleashed a gust strike at it.

It rocked backwards a little bit, but otherwise nothing happened. Sabae scrambled backwards just in time to avoid the statue swinging its stone sword at her. Hugh shuddered at the thought of what the heavy sword might have done.

"They're too heavy to knock back with wind," Sabae said.

Talia grinned. "My turn."

Talia launched a series of dreamfire bolts into the same statue. The effect this time was much more apparent. The first dreamfire bolt cracked the knight statue's chest. The second froze off one side of its face. The third shrank the knight's sword, and the fourth... the fourth set the knight on fire. The burning stone unleashed a plume of foul-smelling smoke, and the knight crumpled to the ground.

"Eat that, you faceless freak!" Talia cackled.

"So... now we've only got a few dozen left to go," Hugh said. He glanced back at Godrick. The rungs he was shaping out of the stone extended a good six feet upwards already.

Talia started pelting more statues with dreamfire bolts, but even at the slow speed they were moving, it took multiple dreamfire bolts to fell each one, and they were

157

already surrounded by the statues. There's no way Talia would be able to hold them all off like that.

Hugh pulled out his sling and another wardstone. He took a deep breath, spun up his sling, and fired the wardstone at a statue carved in the shape of an elderly woman. The statue was actually knocked off its feet, and part of its jaw had been blasted away. None of the nearby statues had been affected, however, and Hugh only had three wardstones left. As he watched, the statue climbed back onto its feet.

"Anyone have a plan?"

"Ah can take them," Godrick called from partway up the wall.

"Not all of them, and not in time," Sabae called back. "Keep working on the ladder."

Talia paused in her barrage, panting.

"There's been something I've been wanting to try for a while now," she said.

She seemed to strain, and then a thin stream of dreamfire projected out of her finger. She used the stream to carve a half circle in front of them, and where it touched, dreamfire licked up from the stone.

Talia let the stream die and focused on the half-circle of dreamfire. The purple-green flames licked up higher, and the line widened to almost three feet thick as she did so.

"I can't hold this up forever," Talia said, "so hurry up, Godrick."

The statues continued advancing on the dreamfire barrier. Their edges seemed to blur and twist, and they seemed to gain a semblance of life in the light of the dreamfire that they'd lacked before.

The first statue, a burly wrestler in a loincloth, reached

the edge of the dreamfire barrier. It paused, slowly jerking its head from side to side to examine the dreamfire. Then it ponderously stepped forwards. As it did so, the dreamfire licked upwards, and the statue began melting-though the drops began falling upwards.

It completely collapsed halfway through the barrier, and the dreamfire rapidly crackled up around it. Talia had begun sweating heavily at this point. More of the statues had reached the edge of the barrier, but most seemed content to wait for it to die down.

Then a large stone bull tried to step across. The dreamfire shattered it before it was halfway across, but more beads of sweat were popping out on Talia's face.

"Hurry up, Godrick," Hugh called.

More and more of the statues tried to cross, but each was destroyed by the dreamfire. By the sixth statue, Talia had collapsed to one knee. Her tattoos had begun to glow.

Then one statue made it across.

The stone ape was burning badly, but it hadn't collapsed yet. It turned to Talia and began to stride towards her. Hugh began to fumble for a wardstone, but Sabae got to the statue first. She punched it right in the cracked center of its chest, and this time she got a reaction. The wind from her strike forced its way deep into the cracks, fueling the dreamfire consuming the ape to much greater heights.

The ape exploded away from Sabae, sending shards of burning stone into the barrier and out into the crowd. Several more statues caught on fire from the shrapnel.

Hugh glanced back up at Godrick. He was over half-way to the tunnel mouth. Just another minute or so should be long enough, he hoped. Godrick looked eerie in the light from the dreamfire, though not as bad as the statues.

Another couple of statues stepped across the barrier. One, an immense stone turtle, collapsed immediately upon stepping out. The other, a stone gorgon (whose snake hair, to Hugh's relief, didn't move on its own), was badly burning, and was blasted to pieces by Sabae in the same way as the ape.

Quite a few statues in the crowd were burning as the dreamfire spread through the crowd now, but more were pressing forwards towards the barrier. Talia was barely holding the barrier up now, and Hugh rushed over to support her and keep her from collapsing onto the ground. Her tattoos were glowing brightly enough that they cast shadows.

"Ah'm almost to the top," Godrick called. "Ye should follow me up now."

Hugh heaved Talia to her feet. He forgot how small she was sometimes, given how much space her personality took up. He started walking her back towards the ladder.

Several more statues stepped across the dying barrier.

"Talia, climb!" Hugh basically lifted her up the ladder. As she slowly started to climb, the dreamfire barrier guttered out, then died entirely, leaving a pit nearly a foot deep in a crescent where the barrier had been. Talia's tattoos dimmed at the same time. The statues that had already been set on fire continued burning, but many of the statues that had been hesitant to cross the fire before had begun advancing on the students.

Sabae hammered apart another burning statue with a gust strike as Hugh started up the ladder after Talia.

"Sabae, let's go!" called Hugh.

Sabae sent out one more windstrike- this one ineffective- and rushed to the ladder. Godrick had already reached the tunnel above them, and was helping Talia up into it.

Hugh was about halfway up when Sabae screamed. Hugh looked down to see that one of the statues, a blindfolded judge, had seized her by the ankle. Hugh frantically reached for his remaining wardstones, but before he could grab them, Godrick's massive sledgehammer hurtled down into the statue's face. Its head crushed, the judge let go of Sabae's ankle and fell to the floor.

Hugh breathed a sigh of relief as Sabae began climbing again. His breath caught when another stone knight began to jerkily lift himself up the ladder. The beheaded judge then stood up and began climbing as well.

"Faster, Sabae!" Hugh called, then began climbing again. Godrick hauled him up into the tunnel when he got there. Hugh collapsed on the floor of the tunnel as Godrick hauled Sabae up. Talia was already lying on the tunnel floor.

"I think my ankle's broken," Sabae said. Godrick moved to look at Sabae's ankle, but Hugh shot up from the floor and grabbed Godrick's shoulder.

"Are they still climbing the ladder?" Hugh asked, walking over to the edge of the tunnel. He looked down to see the knight just a few feet below him. "Godrick, they're climbing the ladder."

Godrick walked over to the edge and smiled. "Ah thought that one out already. It's a lot easier ta destroy than ta create."

Godrick stomped, and the rungs of the ladder fell off the wall one by one from the top down, taking several statues with them. A couple of the statues smashed on hitting the ground, though most survived.

Godrick reached down and summoned his hammer

with a visible effort. It started to rise, but a morbidly obese statue grasped it by the handle and tried to haul it back down. Godrick grunted with the effort of fighting it for the hammer. He looked on the verge of running out of mana when a dreamfire bolt slammed into the statue's shoulder, shattering it. The hammer abruptly flew to Godrick's grasp, nearly knocking him backwards as it did so. The statue's hand was still attached to the handle, and Godrick knocked it off with distaste.

Hugh collapsed against the tunnel wall, panting. They'd made it, somehow.

CHAPTER SIXTEEN

A Fateful Choice

No one moved for several minutes. The only light was coming from the burning statues below, so they were more in shadow than not. Eventually, Hugh hauled himself to his feet and summoned a light cantrip. He looked around their surroundings.

The tunnels of the fifth floor were radically different than the first or sixth floors. Instead of smooth polished granite, the tunnel they were in was rough-hewn sandstone, and barely tall enough for Godrick to stand upright in. Instead of being engraved onto the walls, the ever-present spellforms in the labyrinth were painted on in a flaky white paint. Hugh doubted they were as fragile as they looked, however.

The fifth floor wasn't as quiet as the first, but it was much quieter than the sixth, and most of the noise they were hearing came from the statue room.

Godrick had started tending to Sabae's ankle. They weren't sure if it was broken or just badly sprained, so Godrick chose to just encase Sabae's whole foot in a stone cast, as well as crafting her a stone crutch.

"This is going to slow me down a lot," Sabae said.

"We need ta avoid more battles," Godrick said.

No one answered. Hugh doubted any of them seriously thought that was a possibility. Talia looked like she was barely awake after the amount of mana she'd spent. Even as rich as the Aether was down here, it would take some time for her reservoirs to refill.

"There shouldn't be any sandstone down here," Godrick said. "The mountain's a solid block of granite."

"It's the labyrinth," said Sabae, as though that explained everything.

Maybe it did.

Hugh looked farther down the hallway, and almost yelled in shock. There was something down there. When it didn't move, Hugh eased forwards.

It was a human skeleton, dressed in tattered rags.

This time, Hugh did yell.

Godrick rushed down to his side, lowering his hammer when he saw what it was.

"How long has he been here, do yeh think?" Godrick said.

"A long time, I imagine," Hugh said.

Hugh began to turn away, then spotted something shining. He crouched down to see something shining inside the skeleton's ribcage. He reached in and pulled the object out, dusting it off with his hand.

It was an amulet of some sort. It was only about the width of his thumb, and about half that in length. It consisted of a simple, polished oval stone attached to a silver clasp. A narrow band of silver ran along the border of the stone from the clasp. Incredibly tiny and intricate spellforms ran up and down the clasp and the band. It looked like there had been a cord or leather band that had once held it in place, but it had long since eroded away.

The stone wasn't shiny, or particularly valuable looking. Instead, it was a dull red-orange, almost like the color of brick, with stripes of a dark red brown running across it at an angle just off the horizontal. The lines weren't totally straight, but curved slightly, with gaps between some of them. It looked almost like...

"It's a labyrinth!" Godrick said.

Hugh flipped it over. The back looked almost identical, except that the stone was flat instead of rounded. More spellforms ran down the back of the clasp, which covered the top quarter of the stone's back.

Hugh and Godrick walked back to the others to show them the stone. None of them knew what it did, but they all agreed it had to be enchanted. Hugh tucked it into his belt pouch.

It took them another ten or fifteen minutes before they were ready to move on. Talia still looked exhausted, Godrick wasn't that much better off, and Sabae winced in pain with every step she took. Hugh was the only one still in decent condition.

And even with all the strides forwards as a mage he'd taken in the past few months, Hugh was still mostly useless.

No one looked back into the statue room as they were heading out. No one wanted to.

As they set out, Hugh walked next to Talia.

"We would have died if not for you," he said.

"I'm sure you all would have figured out something," Talia said.

Hugh shook his head. "Godrick's hammer barely slowed those things down, and Sabae couldn't touch them until you'd damaged them. Your dreamfire is really, really powerful, Talia. A regular fire mage wouldn't have been able to do anything to those statues."

Talia blushed a little.

"Alustin knows what he's doing, I guess," was all she said.

No one said anything for a while after that. The increasing number of bones they came across probably had a lot to do with that.

Most of the bones were broken and shattered, and few were human. Most looked like they'd come from various monsters. Hugh began having to step carefully to avoid them. They briefly stopped to consider turning back in hushed whispers, but no one wanted to face the statue room again. They kept on the lookout for a turnoff, but so far they hadn't had any opportunities to take another path.

The four grew more and more tense as they moved down the tunnel. Godrick didn't even curse when he hit his head on the ceiling.

Hugh couldn't help but notice splashes of dried and crumbling brown here and there atop the white paint of the spellforms.

The number of bones had increased to the point where Hugh was about ready to go back and face the statues when the room opened up into a large cavern with two exits. The cavern was big enough that their light cantrips barely reached the far wall, and was absolutely littered with bones. They piled several feet into the air at some points. Stalactites and stalagmites jutted out of the ceiling and floor of the cave.

Hugh glanced at the exits. One exit looked like a continuation of the tunnel they'd been in, while the other was much, much larger.

Godrick gave the cavern a nervous look. "Stalactites an' stalagmites don't form in sandstone," he said.

"That's what you're worrying about?" Talia said irritably.

"It's wrong," Godrick said.

"It's the labyrinth," Sabae said.

"I think we should take the smaller exit," Hugh said. "The big one gives me a bad feeling."

"What did I say about us trusting your gut?" Talia said.

"Ah'm getting a bad feelin' from it too," Godrick said.

"I'm going to say we avoid the bigger exit as well," Sabae said.

"If you're all for it, it's fine by me," Talia said. She poked Hugh in the stomach with a finger. "But if it turns out badly, it's Hugh's gut's fault."

Hugh rubbed his stomach surreptitiously when Talia turned away.

They were about halfway across the cavern when they heard the noise of distant chittering. It was coming from the big exit.

"What is it?" Hugh said. "More imps?"

"Ah don't think so," Godrick said. "Ah don't smell imp. Ah smell… shellfish?"

A swarm of little flying things burst out of the big tunnel. Hugh assumed they were insects at first, but something seemed *wrong* about the way they flew.

Talia launched several dreamfire bolts at the swarm, but had to stop after only a few. Hugh reached for a wardstone, but before he had a chance, the swarm was on them.

They weren't insects, but instead were beetle-winged orange crabs. Hugh yelled as they began biting and pinching his exposed flesh, and he heard the others do the same.

"Get down!" Sabae yelled.

Hugh threw himself downwards just before a massive gust of wind hit him. It launched him across the stone floor until he crashed against a stalagmite rising out of a pile of bones. Flying crabs and more bones pelted against Hugh as the wind continued. He felt himself slipping, and grabbed onto the stalagmite desperately. He slowly felt himself slipping off it, but before his grip was dislodged, the wind died.

Hugh took a second to stand back up. He was covered in bruises and squished crab bits. Sabae was standing looking exhausted, with her palms pressed together over her head where she'd clapped them together. Godrick had managed to grab Talia and sink his sledgehammer into the stone floor. As he watched, Godrick loosened the rock with a spell and it flowed away from the hammer.

"What in the name of the Hundred Clans was that?" Talia asked. She incinerated a single flying crab that had survived the gale.

Sabae looked exhausted. "Uncontrolled release of wind," she said. "The sort of thing I'm supposed to be learning not to do."

Godrick sniffed his shirt. "Hey Hugh, think yeh could do that cleaning cantrip again?"

Hugh started cleaning off the crab guts from their clothing, and passed around the glass scent absorbing sphere. At least he was useful for *something*, he thought bitterly.

They were just getting ready to move on again when something else burst from the big exit. It was another crab, but this one was seven feet tall, and its shell was at least twice that in width. It charged straight at them through the piles of bones.

Talia launched a single dreamfire bolt, which dissolved halfway to the crab. Sabae and Godrick readied themselves- Sabae charging up wind mana in a rapidly constricting sphere around her fist, and Godrick readying his hammer.

Hugh, for once, was ready. He still had his hand in his belt pouch, putting away the glass sphere, so he was able to rapidly pull out a wardstone. He snagged the sling off his belt and spun it up. The crab looked heavily armored, so if he wanted to hurt it he needed to hit some sort of weak spot...

There. The mouth. He just had to get past the twitching crab mouthparts first.

Hugh took a deep breath, aimed, then let loose on his exhale. The wardstone flew straight and true at the crab.

And hit it on the carapace several feet from the mouth.

The blast was enough to put a few cracks in the crab's shell, but it didn't even slow down. Hugh frantically searched for one of his two remaining wardstones, but before he could pull one out of his belt, the crab crashed into Godrick and Sabae.

Sabae's wind punch barely affected the crab, and it sent her flying with the back of a claw. She somehow managed to direct another blast of wind at the floor, arresting her fall.

Godrick's hammer, however, put a massive dent in the crab. Blue ichor dripped out between the cracked shards of the carapace.

The crab, unfortunately, was far from dead. It knocked him over with another backhand from a claw, and the huge youth rolled into a pile of bones. He managed to get his hammer up in time to block another blow from the crab claw, but he wasn't able to block the crab's leg striking at him. It pierced directly into Godrick's leg, and he screamed, dropping his hammer and grabbing at the crab's offending limb.

The crab opened its claw, reaching down for Godrick.

Time seemed to slow to a stop. Hugh's grasping hand found one of the last two wardstones, and he started pulling it out of the belt pouch, feeling as though he were swimming through honey.

Beside him, Talia screamed wordlessly, and her tattoos flashed to life.

And the bones beneath the crab began to grow.

It looked like flames made of bone were rising out of the scattered bones on the floor, but at close to the speed of an arrow shot. The flame-shaped bones impacted the base of the crab's carapace. They pierced the shell in several places, and actually *lifted* the entire crab off the ground. Godrick was lifted as the crab's leg rose, until the crab's leg slipped out of his thigh. He screamed in pain as he fell back to the ground.

After a few seconds, the bones stopped growing, leaving an enraged crab trapped in a massive bone outcrop. It started flailing its claws wildly, battering at the bone outcrop.

Cracks started to form in the bone, but not from the claw's actions. They were starting at the base and growing upwards. And they were *glowing*, like the embers in a hearth.

169

"Get Godrick away from there," Talia said, and collapsed.

Hugh briefly stepped towards her, then turned and ran towards Godrick. He managed to get Godrick standing on his one good leg somehow, and started helping him hobble away. He could feel heat emanating from the bone outcrop, until it started to feel like standing near a furnace.

"Get out of here, Hugh," Godrick said. "Ah'll be fine."

Hugh ignored him, and kept helping Godrick forwards.

"Hugh, ah…" Godrick started.

"No," Hugh said, and kept helping. The heat had grown to the point where it was almost painful, and he could hear a loud cracking noise behind them.

Godrick looked behind them. "Get down," he yelled, and tackled Hugh onto the ground.

Just in time for the entire bone outcrop to violently explode.

Even under Godrick, Hugh felt a violent wash of heat and pressure, and he felt several shards of bone slice along the skin of his arm. He blacked out for a moment, but when he came to shards of bone and bits of crab were still pattering down onto the ground.

"You can get off me now, Godrick," Hugh said.

Godrick didn't say anything.

"Godrick?"

Scared now, Hugh managed to wriggle out from underneath Godrick's bulk. He gasped when he saw Godrick's back.

Godrick's shirt was burnt clean off his back, and a number of shards of bone jutted out of his skin, including one that had at least six inches jutting out of his back, with who knows how much inside him. The skin on Godrick's back was horribly burnt, and even charred in places.

Hugh was worried that Godrick was dead for a moment, until he saw Godrick's back shift as he took a breath.

"NO!" Sabae hobbled over to Hugh and Godrick as fast as she could in the stone cast, falling to her knees beside Godrick.

"He's still alive, but I don't know for how much longer," Hugh said worriedly.

Sabae was crying now. She reached out towards Godrick, but stopped before she touched his back.

"No," Sabae said quietly.

She reached out with both hands and planted them solidly on Godrick's back. She took a deep breath, and then her hands began to *glow.*

Hugh took a step back in shock. Lines of light spread out across Godrick's back. Godrick's burns receded as the lines passed them, and bits of bone were forced out of the wounds as they closed. Even the big shard of bone forced itself out of his back, revealing a terrifying length of bone that had been embedded in Godrick.

The lines of light shot down to Godrick's leg, clustering around the hole that went through it. It started to knit itself together.

Then the light simply went out, and Sabae fell backwards.

Godrick hadn't been completely healed, but it looked like his breath was coming much more easily now. His bleeding had lessened, but he looked stable. Sabae sat up and gave Hugh a despairing look.

"I said I'd never use my healing affinity," she said.

"You just saved your friend's life," Hugh said. "There's nothing for you to be ashamed of."

"It doesn't matter," Sabae said. "We're all going to die down here anyways."

Hugh didn't say anything. He glanced over at Talia, who was stirring on the ground.

He felt rage bubble up inside of him. Not at the crab monster, or the statues, or even Rhodes, without whom they'd never have been dropped down here. No.

The rage was targeted at himself.

Hugh was still useless. He could craft a ward or put together a cantrip, but when it really counted, he couldn't protect himself or his friends.

Hugh turned and stomped off. He pumped more mana into the light cantrip drifting at his side, until it was so bright it almost hurt to look at.

"Hugh?" Sabae said.

Hugh ignored her, and stomped over to the big exit. He strode a few paces down it. The tunnel quickly opened into another, smaller cavern with no other exits, and no crabs that he could see alive in there. There was a shallow pool of water with what looked like egg-sacks in it, however.

Hugh stomped back out to the others.

"There's no crabs left in that side cave, and it looks more defensible than this one."

Talia had limped over to them.

"What's the point?" Sabae muttered. "We're not going to make it out of here."

"You never give up," Talia said. "You haven't failed until you do."

Sabae looked up at the two of them, then simply nodded.

Somehow, between the three of them, they managed to haul the unconscious Godrick into the side cave. The instant they had cleared the bones from a patch of ground and laid Godrick into it, Talia and Sabae passed out next to him. Hugh thought briefly about waking one of them to keep helping, but dismissed the thought.

They were the ones who'd done everything to help save them, while Hugh had done nothing. Hugh slipped his spellbook off his shoulder and got to work.

The first thing he did was anchor several light cantrips on various stalactites and stalagmites, so that the cavern was well lit.

Hugh started piling up the larger bones at the narrowest point of the entrance to the side cavern. It took him hours, but he eventually managed to construct a barricade of interlocking bones across the entrance. He doubted it would keep out any really determined creatures, but it was better than nothing.

He attended to the pond next. He tested the water with a simple cantrip. It wasn't the cleanest, but it wouldn't poison them. He refilled all of their water bottles.

His gaze turned to the crab eggs, and his eyes narrowed.

On the spot, a cantrip seemed to assemble itself in his mind's eye. It was essentially just a basic levitation cantrip, remarkably like the first one he'd ever successfully cast, but much, much more carefully targeted.

Carefully, so as not to break any, he slowly levitated all of the eggs onto the shore of the pond. He then picked up a femur, and systematically obliterated every single egg. He smashed the gelatinous spheres over and over again with the bone, splattering himself and his surroundings with their foul-smelling contents.

After a while, the femur cracked, and Hugh threw it to the ground. The others somehow hadn't woken up from the noise.

Hugh started searching the room for any treasure like the amulet he'd found on the skeleton earlier.

There wasn't much- the crabs didn't seem to be intelligent, so any treasure that ended up in here did so largely by accident. He found a few gold coins, an enchanted dagger, and a shield so badly battered Hugh doubted its enchantment worked.

Once he was done with that, he reinforced the barricade some more, and crafted some wards behind it to further shield them.

Then he cleaned all the crab ichor and bits off of himself and his friends, using the little glass sphere to remove the stench as well.

Then he just sat down by the pond. He looked around for something else to do, but there was nothing else.

So he just sat there with his thoughts.

Hugh really was worthless. He hadn't been able to help his friends at all. His wardstones had proven to just be useless trinkets, especially given that he had been dumb enough to not have a way to easily have them on hand, just putting them in his belt pouch. When the statues had attacked, he couldn't do anything, and the other three had to save him. When the crabs attacked, the same thing happened. Hugh did nothing but hold the team back.

If Hugh hadn't been with them in the first place, they never would have gotten into this mess. Rhodes wouldn't have gotten so angry and started the fight, and they never would have fallen down here.

When danger came, his friends had stood up to the challenge. Talia had used her bone affinity for the first time to save them from the crab. Godrick had literally thrown himself in front of an explosion for Hugh. Sabae had broken her vow not to use her healing for Godrick.

Hugh, though? Hugh was just dead weight.

A little voice in the back of Hugh's head tried to remind him of the levitation spell he'd cast that had saved his friends, but he ignored it.

The longer Hugh sat there, the angrier and angrier he got at himself. He hated himself like he'd never hated anyone before- not his aunt, not his uncle, not his obnoxious cousins, not his uncaring teachers before Alustin, not Rhodes. The world would be better off without someone like him. Nothing good came out of a mage from Emblin.

His anger grew and grew, and Hugh felt like it was going to explode out of him, until, all of a sudden, it just... drained away.

Hugh burst into tears.

Hugh had no idea how long it had been when he finally stopped crying. He just felt empty and broken inside. His friends were going to die, and there was nothing he could do. Hugh was a worthless piece of nothing.

He looked over at them, and then narrowed his eyes.

No. There was one thing he could do.

He padded over beside their sleeping forms, but didn't wake them. Instead, he grabbed his spellbook and strode over to the pond.

He sat down on the shore of the underground pond and stared at the book in his lap for a moment, then looked up at the pond.

It was... actually kind of beautiful. Hugh had no idea how long they'd been in the labyrinth, but it felt like it must have been at least a day already. Hugh was bone tired. Every muscle in his body ached, and he had cuts and bruises everywhere. Even a burn on one hand that he had no memory of acquiring.

For all the horrors of the labyrinth, the pond was peaceful. Gentle ripples reflected the light from his cantrip onto the ceiling of the cave, and he spent quite a while just watching the patterns the light reflected on the ceiling.

Eventually, though, he took a deep breath and unlatched his spellbook. He slowly rifled through the pages, carefully inspecting the notes on the various wards he'd constructed in the short weeks since his birthday. When he got to the blank pages, he moved a little faster, but still couldn't force himself to turn them with any urgency.

Eventually, however, he reached a page near the back of the book. A page where he'd drawn a warlock contract he'd taken from a book of forbidden rituals.

There was a way he could help his friends, and all it would cost him was a deal with a demon.

"Bakori. Bakori. Ba…"

CHAPTER SEVENTEEN

The Contract

Before Hugh could finish saying Bakori's name a third time, something slipped out of the back of the spellbook and brushed his hand. His voice caught in his throat.

They were just three blank pages of paper, but Hugh suddenly felt hope rise in his heart.

They were pages he'd torn out from an Index Node in the Grand Library.

Hugh slowly pulled out the pages from the back of the spellbook, his hands shaking. He stared at them, warlock contract completely forgotten.

The index pages had the ability to lead you to any book in the library collection.

The pages could show Hugh and his friends the way out of the Labyrinth.

Hugh desperately scrambled for a quill and inkpot. He got them out and slammed the spellbook shut, using it as a writing desk.

His hands were shaking so hard he splattered ink across the page. He couldn't think of what to write for a moment, then smiled.

72 Uses of Dragon Dung.

The page did nothing for a moment, and Hugh's heart felt like it was going to stop. Abruptly, however, the page lifted up into the air and began to fold itself. It felt like it took forever, but when it was done, a simple crane hovered in the air in front of Hugh.

The crane darted out over the pond, circled back, flew over Hugh's sleeping friends, then flew back to Hugh.

Then, to Hugh's despair, the page unfolded itself and landed atop the book. On it was written two short sentences.

Current location unknown. Unable to locate requested volume.

Hugh's hopes crumpled. He angrily threw the pages to one side and stared at the warlock contract again.

He should have known there was no other way out of this. There'd be no easy solution for Hugh the Worthless.

Hugh took a deep breath and prepared to summon Bakori.

Then he stopped, and his eyes flicked back to the

Index pages lying on the shore next to him.

Then his eyes flicked back to the contract.

Then back to the pages.

A tiny spark of hope appeared in Hugh's heart again.

Hugh frantically snatched up the pages from the beach again.

What was it that Alustin had said on the day of the Choosing, when he first told Hugh he was a warlock?

Warlocks could pact with any sentient being.

Or any being with the capacity to become sentient.

And Alustin had told them that the Index was already semisentient.

He wet his quill in his inkpot again, and set it to the page below **Unable to locate selected volume.**

Are you still connected to the rest of the Index?
I am the Index.
I mean, is this page still linked to the Index?
Yes, though some directional functionality remains limited.

Hugh took a deep breath before setting his quill to paper again.

I want to form a warlock pact with you.

There was no reply immediately. Hugh waited for what felt like eternity, even though it must have only been a few seconds. His heart started to sink, convinced this was a waste of time.

Then, finally, new words appeared.

You want *what?*

Hugh smiled.

I want to form a warlock pact with the Index.
One moment. Processing unique request.

Hugh waited impatiently. It took almost a minute before the page responded again. The letters this time appeared bolder, and appeared to have a little more life to them. If Hugh was going to try and describe the emotions of letters, he'd say they looked shocked.

Why would you possibly want to form a warlock pact with the Index?
I'm an apprentice who got trapped in one of the lower levels of the labyrinth by accident while taking my final test for the year. My teammates are wounded and exhausted, and me gaining affinities from a warlock pact is the only chance of us making it out of here alive.
…Who is this? Attempting to prank or confuse the Index is a serious violation of Library rules.
My name is Hugh of Emblin. My teammates are Sabae Kaen Das, Talia of Clan Castis, and Godrick, son of Artur Wallbreaker. I'm not trying to prank you. We're trapped on the fifth level of the labyrinth- if the demon who tried to get me to sign a warlock contract with him was telling the truth, that is- and though we have a temporary safe spot, who knows how long it will last.
…Demon?
It's a bit of a long story, but yes, there's a demon named Bakori wandering around down here who has offered me the power to save my friends, but I'd really rather not sign a contract with a demon.
Understandable. Contracts with demons tend to

turn out very, very badly.

Hugh was starting to suspect that the Index was a little more than semi-sentient, as Alustin had called it.

This is… an exceptionally unusual request. Give me a few minutes while I verify your story.

Hugh leaned back and allowed himself to smile.
That wasn't a no.

It took quite some time for the Index to respond again. Hugh wasn't sure how long, but eventually more words scrawled across the page.

Your story checks out. The four of you were reported to have fallen, but scrying attempts for you over the last day have all failed- a normal result when attempting to scry the labyrinth. Your status as a warlock is by no means common knowledge, so it seems improbable that it could be anyone other than you.
So you'll sign a contract with me?
Normally I would simply say no, but in this case, I feel circumstances might demand it. I must ask one question first, however.

Hugh's heart felt like it was going to stop when the Index wrote no, but it promptly started back up again when the sentence completed.

Anything.
Why do you seek to pact with me?

To save my friends.

There was to response for a moment.
Very well.

Hugh sighed in relief.

Let's do this, then! I...
No. I'm willing to pact with you, but not without firmly establishing terms and conditions first.
Like what?

Nothing happened for a moment, then a long list started writing itself, actually wrapping over to the next page.

The signer of this contract confirms that they truly are Hugh of Emblin. If a party other than Hugh of Emblin signs this contract, the contract will enforce itself fatally upon them.
Hugh of Emblin will not knowingly put the Index, the Library, or the staff of the Library in danger if it is at all possible to avoid. Violation of this clause is room for declaring the contract null and void. Severe enough violations may be grounds for enforcing this contract fatally.
Hugh of Emblin will be responsible for bringing at least one (1) volume to be added to the Library's collection each year. Said volume must not be already possessed by the Library. If Hugh of Emblin fails to do so, that will be allowable cause for declaring the contract null and void. Reasonable accommodation will be

made for this requirement, however- for example, if Hugh of Emblin is traveling and will have difficulty returning to the Library on time, or is ill, or if similar extenuating circumstances occur.

The contract went on and on like that for some time. All told, there were nearly thirty clauses to the contract, establishing allowable behavior, requirements, and the like. At the very end was a single clause that simply read:

Hugh of Emblin will have his mana intermingled with the drafting party of this contract, and will be granted appropriate affinities thereby, as well as training in how to use them.

Hugh smiled and put his pen to paper.

I accept.

Hugh pulled out the second sheet of Index paper and began to copy the contract he'd recorded in his spellbook onto it. He drew a series of spellforms linking the clauses on the first page with the contract, then linked it all together.

The last step was actually signing it. It didn't require actually signing the contract, or signing it in blood, like some imaginative story-tellers had claimed. Instead, it simply required both parties to channel their mana into the two unlinked portions of the contract's spellforms. Normally both parties needed to be physically present, but since they were writing the contract on paper that was physically part of the Index, Hugh was sure that it would work fine.

Hugh took a deep breath and reached his finger towards the spot he needed to touch. Then a single word scrawled itself across the page.

No.

The page jerked itself out of Hugh's hands, flew out over the pond, and ignited. It burned to ash in seconds, which drifted down into the pond.

Hugh stared at the pond in shock, then down at the pages in his hands. Words were writing themselves onto the first sheet below the clauses.

That contract spellform is intended for contracts with demons. Where did you find that? Was it from the demon Bakori you mentioned?

Hugh quickly wrote down the story about finding the volume of forbidden spells.

Fascinating. I have no record of that book. That book should not be shelved there, and should be in a much more secure section. This is a mystery for another time, however. Given the danger of your situation, we should complete your contract quickly. I will provide the contract spellform. Once the contract is complete, you and your friends need to STAY WHERE YOU ARE. I will send help for you. That being said, know that I sign this contract against my better judgment. If there were any other way to locate you, I would take it, but signing a contract might be the only way to find you.

Hugh watched, fascinated, as a new spellform sketched itself on the final page in his possession. It largely resembled the first contract, but it had a number of key differences, most notably in the manner in which energy was routed between the signatories. In a matter of minutes, the new warlock contract was done, and the empty spellform for the Index's magical signature lit up.

Hugh took a deep breath, trying to calm his racing heart, and pressed his finger against the page, then channeled his mana through it.

Hugh's world went white.

Hugh was sitting in a blank, empty void, with only whiteness surrounding him. He was naked, holding only the warlock contract and the page with the clauses in his hand. He opened his mouth to speak, but before he could say anything, the letters and spellforms began tearing themselves out of the page. They drifted and swirled like a cloud of bugs in front of him for a moment.

Hugh reached out to touch the letters, but the instant he touched one, it burned his skin, leaving a welt. He pulled his hand back, hissing.

And then all the letters and spellforms shot straight at him like arrows.

Each and every one burned worse than anything he'd ever felt before, and he could feel them crawling beneath his skin, writhing and twisting and rewriting themselves. The pain felt like it would last forever, but then it stopped.

Hugh panted, barely conscious. He looked down and saw the spellforms seemed to have tattooed himself on his chest. Even as he watched, the blisters and welts faded away to nothing. He could feel writing on his back as well, and somehow knew it was the contract's clauses.

Slowly, the tattooed contract began to fade. So did the white void around him.

But it wasn't replaced by the cave.

Instead, Hugh found himself being swept up by a mighty river. He couldn't tell which way was up, and found himself being pulled every which way by the powerful currents. His lungs burned, and he frantically tried to swim through the water, only to have it turn into skin tearing wind, and then a suffocating flow of sand, and then writhing vines, and…

"Hugh!"

The vision went on and on, and the powerful forces tearing at him never relented, and never held a single form for longer than a moment.

"Hugh, wake up!"

Finally, just when he thought he was about to succumb to the current, he felt something immensely strong grab him by the arm and haul him out of it.

Awaken, Hugh. Your friends need you.

CHAPTER EIGHTEEN

Something Hungry This Way Comes

Hugh woke with a gasp. He felt… different. He could feel his mana reservoirs like he never could before. There were three new, deep channels leading into and out of them. He…

He sat up abruptly, only to be hit by a blinding pain. He recoiled, only to realize a second later that he'd smacked Talia in the forehead with his own forehead.

"Hugh! You're awake!" Talia tackled Hugh, knocking him back down to the ground and squeezing him so hard that he thought his ribs would break. "We all woke up and you were asleep and having some sort of nightmare and there were spellforms glowing on your chest and we couldn't wake you for hours and…" Talia pulled out of the hug and looked Hugh deep in the eyes, her face inches away from his.

Then she slapped him. Really, really hard.

"What in the name of the ghosts of everyone who ever froze to death did you do to yourself? You had us all scared senseless!"

Talia smacked him upside the head, and Hugh raised his arms to protect himself.

At which point Talia punched him in the stomach. "I thought you cared enough not to worry us like that, Hugh! I…"

A hand reached out and caught Talia's arm before she could hit Hugh again. Sabae bodily picked up Talia, turned away, and set her on her feet.

"What Talia means to say," Sabae said, "is that we're all very concerned and would like to know what happened after we fell asleep."

Sabae offered Hugh a hand up, and as she helped him stand Hugh got a chance to look around for the first time since he'd woken up. He was still in the cave, still by the pond. He had no idea how much time had passed, but…

It was at that point that Sabae wrapped him in a hug, and he realized how much stronger physically she was than Talia.

"Can't breathe. Can't…"

Sabae let him go, and he took a deep breath of the cool

cave air in relief.

"Where's mah hug?" Hugh heard Godrick say. Hugh turned around to see Godrick propped sitting up against a stalagmite near the shore. Hugh smiled, happy to see Godrick awake, and strode over towards him. He paused just out of hugging range, however.

"Please don't break my ribs, Godrick," he said.

"Don't think ah can right now, honestly," Godrick said.

Hugh leaned in and hugged Godrick. True to his word, Godrick's hug was gentle- for Godrick, at least. Hugh was sure he'd hardly gotten more than a few bruises from it.

The others joined them, and they all sat looking at the pond.

"I signed a warlock contract," Hugh said.

Everyone's heads snapped to look at him.

"Why would you…" Godrick started.

"Not with that demon?" Sabae said at the same time.

Talia just growled inarticulately at him.

"No, I didn't sign a contract with the demon. I signed it with the Index, and I did it to try and save all of you."

Everyone was silent for a moment, and then Talia spoke up.

"You did WHAT?"

It took Hugh quite a while to explain what had happened, after which they were silent for a time.

"What affinities did yeh get?" Godrick asked.

"I…" Hugh said. "I, uh, don't actually know."

Everyone stared at him.

"You don't know?" Sabae said.

"I didn't think to ask," Hugh said.

"You didn't think to ask?" Sabae said.

Hugh didn't know what to say to that.

"I, uh… I think I have three of them," Hugh said.

"Well, uh… that's nothin' ta sneer at," Godrick said.

"I bet you have an affinity for sheer idiocy," Talia said.

Hugh dodged an elbow from Talia, but she didn't seem to be trying that hard to hit him this time.

"So now all we have to do is wait," Sabae said.

"After all of this, I'm fine with being patient for once," Talia said.

Everyone looked at her in surprise.

"I can be patient when I want. What? Quit looking at me like that!"

They waited for hours and hours without anything happening. They talked for much of that time- of Talia's figuring out her bone affinity on her own, of Sabae's reluctant decision that she should learn to properly use her healing affinity, and of Godrick's desire to simply finish attuning fully, so he'd never find himself so vulnerable again.

Hugh gave the enchanted dagger to Talia and the shield (which probably didn't work) to Sabae. He offered an apology to Godrick for not having anything for him, but Godrick just laughed and said it was fine.

Finally, Hugh found the nerve to talk about what had been lurking at the back of his head for so long.

"I'm sorry I've been a burden for so long," Hugh said. "If I'd had a pact before, maybe I actually could have helped you out more in the tunnels, instead of just being a useless burden."

Everyone stared at him for a moment, and then Talia slapped him in the face again. Even harder than before.

"You're not a burden, you great idiot!" Talia said.

Hugh rubbed his cheek. "I wasn't able to help you all like I should, and maybe you wouldn't have been hurt if I..."

"Talia's right, you really are an idiot," Sabae said. "You're the last thing from a burden. If it hadn't been for your wardstones, we would have taken a lot more in the way of injuries from those imps on the first level. And you saved all of our lives when you stopped our fall down that shaft."

"If it hadn't been for you basically hauling me up Godrick's ladder," Talia said, "I doubt I would have gotten out of the statue room."

"Ah would have died when Talia's bone outcropping exploded if yeh hadn't hauled me away from it, Hugh. Yeh saved my life," Godrick said.

"Hugh, we all depended on each other out there," Sabae said. "If any of us had been absent, none of us would have survived- and that includes you. You need to stop thinking of yourself as worthless, Hugh. You're one of the smartest mages I know, and I'm happy to have you by my side."

"Aye," said Godrick.

"I'm going to beat you black and blue next time I hear one of your damn speeches about how worthless you are, Hugh," Talia said. "They might be the most annoying thing I know."

Hugh grinned weakly and tried to surreptitiously wipe the corner of his eye. The others, thankfully, pretended not to notice.

"Thank you all so much for everything," Hugh said. "I..."

It was at that point that they heard a crunch come from

beyond the bone barrier, and then something enormous growling.

Everyone went immediately silent. Hugh cursed himself silently. He'd assumed that they were safe just because he'd gotten in touch with help when he pacted with the Index. He'd just let them all yammer on like fools, even knowing that if a monster down here overheard them it could mean their deaths.

The thing on the other side of the barricade brushed against it, and several bones came clattering down. Hugh could hear the thing breathing raggedly.

To his sides, Hugh could see Talia's tattoos begin to glow, and wind begin to circle around Sabae's fists. Godrick's fingers began to sink down into the stone below him.

The barricade shuddered again, and Talia's tattoos brightened even farther. The bones of the barricade began to rapidly grow, filling the hallway. The glowing cracks followed soon behind. If the creature stayed there, maybe...

The barrier shattered as *something* plunged through it. Hugh's wards detonated, not seeming to affect the creature at all. The extra bone that Talia had grown exploded when it was broken, and the thing was lost in the flame for a moment. It rolled across the ground, putting much of the fire out, and climbed onto its feet again.

It looked like a wolf, if wolves were ten feet tall, covered in scales, and had writhing mouths full of fangs running down their sides. The creature looked around the room for a moment, then fixed its gaze on them.

Then it charged.

Time seemed to slow down for Hugh again. He could

190

see Talia launching dreamfire bolts at the creature to one side, and Sabae readying herself behind her new shield. Several spikes of stone shot up from the floor in front of the creature, but it slammed through them without slowing down or seemingly being injured.

Hugh found himself desperately reaching out with his hands and his mind, and his mind... found something. It latched itself onto one of the new channels running through his mana reservoirs, and redirected the flow outwards. Hugh didn't even try to craft a spellform in his mind's eye- he just let the torrent of mana flow through him, and somehow felt the Aether ripple around him as he did so.

A shaft of molten light tore out of Hugh's hands, slamming right into the charging beast's chest. The air seemed to scream, and waves of heat slammed into Hugh.

The creature simply exploded, splattering across the room in a wave of gore and ichor.

The light blinked out. Hugh stared at his hands for a moment, then looked at his friends in shock.

And promptly fainted.

CHAPTER NINETEEN

An Unexpected Conversation

The first thing Hugh noticed upon waking up was that the rock floor of the cavern was oddly soft.

The second thing he noticed is that he didn't remember there being blankets in the cave.

Hugh opened his eyes and bolted upright. He was in an unfamiliar bed in an empty room, with a whole row of beds next to him. Only one was occupied, however. In it lay Godrick, who was heavily bandaged and asleep.

"It's about time you woke up," someone said.

Hugh turned away from Godrick to see Alustin, who was sitting on a chair nearby, reading a book. In fact, he hadn't actually looked up from the book at all- he was still reading.

"Sir, what…" Hugh started.

"How many times do I have to ask you to call me Alustin?" Alustin said.

"Sir, what happened? How did I… we… get here? Where are Sabae and Talia? Why…" Hugh said in a rush.

Alustin held up his hand without looking away from his book, stopping Hugh in his tracks. "Sabae and Talia are fine, they're merely in the girl's wing of the infirmary. As for the rest of your questions, I'll answer them- and many more, I'm sure- in a moment. For now, though, get dressed, and I'll meet you in the hallway. We have somewhere to be."

Alustin reached under his chair and tossed a student uniform onto the bed, then left the room, still reading as he

192

walked. Hugh noticed his spellbook, beltpouch, and Clan Castis dagger were all tucked between the trousers, shirt, and jacket.

Hugh quickly got dressed and followed Alustin out the door.

Alustin tucked his book into his ever-present satchel as Hugh walked into the hallway, and gestured for Hugh to follow him.

"Before I answer any more questions, I'm going to need to hear your version of events down in the caverns," Alustin said.

Hugh told him everything. About the imps on the first floor, the fight with Rhodes, the encounter with Bakori the demon, the statues, the crabs, and the horrid wolf creature.

Alustin was quiet for several minutes, then finally sighed. During that time, Hugh recognized where they were- they were heading towards the library.

"Ask your questions, Hugh."

"What happened down in the labyrinth after I passed out?" Hugh asked. "The last thing I remember was blasting apart that wolf creature with… fire? I pacted with the Index, I was expecting a paper affinity or something."

Alustin sighed. "You tapped into a brand new, completely unattuned affinity, then cast an unstructured spell that not only used up your entire mana reserves, but also drained much of the mana from the Aether immediately surrounding you. It badly overstressed your mana channels and reservoirs, as well as giving you significant burns all over your hands and arms."

Hugh glanced at his hands. They seemed fine.

"We- that being Artur Wallbreaker, Aedan Dragonslayer, Sulassa Tidecaller, and a few others- arrived less than an hour after you slew the… we have no idea what it was, considering how little of it you left behind, and your friends' descriptions didn't shed a lot of light on it. We brought you out of the labyrinth, and you've been recovering ever since. You were unconscious for about two days, even with all the healing magic the infirmary healers have been pumping into you."

They passed into the library, and began heading down the stairs towards the restricted sections. Hugh realized that Alustin had never actually answered the question about his new affinity.

"It's astonishing that you survived as long as you did down there, Hugh. No one has ever heard of a group of first years that made it down that deep and lived to tell the tale. Most full mages seldom venture much deeper than you went. You were extremely lucky- but you also had help."

"Help?" Hugh said, but he had a suspicion he knew what Alustin was about to say.

Alustin didn't say anything, though. Instead, he walked up to a door, and pressed his hand against a spellform on it. The door cracked open, and on the other side was the immense, cavernous space of the Grand Library.

"Sir, should I be here? You spent all that time warning us about how dangerous it is…"

"You're with me, you'll be fine. Besides, your contracted partner is here, and you need to meet them in person."

They strode out onto the balcony, and Alustin walked them to the nearest index node. He wrote something Hugh didn't see, and the page tore itself out, folding itself into a tiny pegasus in mid-air. Hugh and Alustin followed it as it took off along the balcony.

John Bierce

"Sir, where are we…"

"I've been lying to you for some time, Hugh." Alustin looked somewhat ashamed as he said this.

"Sir?"

"Hugh, when's the last time you've gone outside of the mountain?" Alustin said.

"…Sir?" Hugh replied, genuinely puzzled.

"When's the last time you went outside?" Alustin said.

"Uhhh… I couldn't say for sure, but it's been a while, sir," Hugh said. "I've been pretty busy training for the labyrinth test."

"When exactly?" Alustin said.

Hugh started to open his mouth, then closed it, puzzled. The pegasus flew out into the immense open space in the center of the room, where a large platform assembled itself out of flying cobblestones in midair. It was big enough for a dozen people, so Hugh and Alustin fit easily. The instant they stepped on board, the whole thing began to descend.

"I… I'm not sure," Hugh said.

Alustin gave him a serious look.

"So far as anyone in Skyhold knows, you have not once set foot outside of the mountain since you entered it. You've skipped every class with a field trip and always found ways to dodge going outside with your friends."

Hugh wracked his brain, and realized to his dismay that he actually couldn't think of a single time he'd gone outside since he'd gotten to Skyhold. How had that happened? Hugh loved the outdoors, and had spent most of his childhood in the woods of Emblin.

Alustin pulled a series of rolled-up drawings out of his satchel and handed them to Hugh. Hugh opened them up as they passed a floor that seemed to be entirely filled with books made of glass.

"Sir, these are my wards from my room… and from my old room, too."

"What do the spellforms in blue do, Hugh?"

"They… uh… hmmm."

Hugh couldn't remember what those spellforms did, even though he distinctly remembered adding them to his room wards.

"They're wards meant to protect your dreams from outside intrusion, Hugh."

Hugh stared at Alustin.

"Why would I draw those, and why didn't I know what they were?"

Alustin was silent for a moment.

"Do you remember the first time I told you that you were a warlock, Hugh?"

"Yes," Hugh said cautiously.

"Do you remember that I told you that if I'd even suspected you'd been in contact with a demon, that I'd have taken drastic measures?"

"Yes," Hugh said cautiously again. "But I wasn't, so you didn't."

"I lied," said Alustin. "You have, in fact, been in contact with a demon since the first day you walked into Skyhold."

Hugh stared at Alustin in shock as the platform continued to slowly descend through the immense chamber.

"I… no I haven't, sir!" Hugh said.

"You have indeed, Hugh, though not consciously. Uncontracted warlocks are particularly susceptible to mental manipulation by potential contracting partners.

Demons are especially fond of doing so, and by doing so gaining the services of warlocks. Since you first set foot in Skyhold the demon you met below has been subtly manipulating you in an effort to gain a contracted warlock."

Hugh looked away from Alustin and stared out into the space in the center of the immense room. A huge bridge spanned the nearest corner of the room on this level, and it was entirely filled with rows and rows of bookshelves.

"The demon Bakori was the reason that you never left the mountain. If you had, you would have left the range of his mental manipulation, and who knows if you would have willingly returned," Alustin said. "He was the reason you kept isolating yourself socially farther and farther."

"I've always been shy and bad with people," Hugh said. "He didn't make me that way."

"No, but he exacerbated the problem," Alustin said. "He amplified your feelings of loneliness, your despair at your inability to do magic, all of it. All to make you more vulnerable. It was Bakori that led you to the library door with the weakened wards, and Bakori that led you to the volume of forbidden spells in here, not the Index."

Hugh watched an origami golem in the shape of a seagull desperately flap to get away from a pack of hungry grimoires pursuing it through the air. He felt a little sick as he thought about all the gut feelings that kept leading him astray over the last year.

"Once you entered the labyrinth itself, the demon's manipulation grew much more overt. Those gut feelings that led you down specific pathways? Those came from Bakori," Alustin said.

"Sir, maybe you should stop saying his name so much, so you don't draw his attention," Hugh said.

Alustin smiled, but there was no humor to it.

"There's no risk of that, Hugh. You were the only one who he could hear calling his name, and only because of the spells he had placed on you, and those were all broken when you signed a warlock pact. Not many spells can survive that sort of interference."

The blue-white glow from below was growing close now, bathing the lower levels of the room in its light. It didn't seem like they could have dropped that far at the speed they were going, but they had to be miles below the level near the top of the room where they had started.

"It was Bakori who led you to that secret chamber above the mana flume chamber where you found him," Alustin said. "Rhodes was manipulated there as well, but by swarms of Bakori's imps instead. In retrospect, the test should have been stopped as soon as students started reporting imps showing up. It's amazing we didn't have any deaths this year. It was Bakori who amplified your despair as you fought your way through the labyrinth, and it seems Bakori almost had you in that last cavern. But…"

Alustin didn't say anything for a moment.

"But?" Hugh said.

"You fought back," Alustin said. "You've been fighting back this whole time."

"I've been what?"

"You've been fighting back," Alustin repeated.

Hugh could see indistinct shapes in the glow below them. They were orderly, regular, and shifting constantly.

"You might not have consciously known you were being manipulated, but you did subconsciously- and you were fighting it to the point that you were unknowingly drawing wards on your door to try and keep Bakori out of your dreams. In fact, your unusual abilities with wards might be directly related to this- I've never heard of a warlock whose will imbuing abilities apply to wardcrafting. The vast majority of warlocks have those talents apply elsewhere- battle magic, bindings, or banishments, usually. Your subconscious might have forced your will imbuing abilities to apply to your wards in order to help protect you from the demon."

Hugh thought back to the fight he and Talia had when she found his lair, and the nightmares he had the night before he repaired his wards. He found himself nodding slowly. Then a thought occurred to him.

"How do you know all of this, sir?"

"Much of it I've pieced together from circumstantial evidence and the stories of others. I do have to admit, however, than I have been, uh… spying on you for some time. One of my attunements is farseeing."

Hugh stared at Alustin in surprise. He'd never told his apprentices what his attunements were, though they'd suspected he had more than one. Farseeing, however, was a rare attunement for a battle mage. It was closely related to light attunements, but rather than manipulating light, allowed the mage to see visions of far away places- or, at the least, see long distances. It was a highly valued power, but extremely difficult to train and use.

"Was the demon why you haven't told us what your attunements are? What are your others?"

Alustin just smiled and pointed off the side of the platform.

"This is the Index."

They were sinking down into the blue haze. Hugh was sure there was no way that they had approached so closely so fast, but the air was already glowing misty around them.

The haze itself wasn't any particular color- it just looked like incredibly thick mist. The blue glow came from the moving shapes inside the mist. As they drew closer, he reached out and ran his hand through the mist. He could feel a slight resistance, but he doubted he would have noticed it if he hadn't been paying attention.

As they sunk fully into it, Hugh could start to make out shapes within it. Gears, chains, axles, and more arched around them through the mist. They turned, ratcheted, and shifted all about them. They all seemed to be made of brilliant blue light, though Hugh couldn't get a good look at any through the mist. Tiny blue sparks darted about the mists. Whenever Hugh tried to watch one its behavior looked random, but when he looked at the movement of the sparks as a swarm, the order of their behavior became immediately obvious, though he doubted he could explain it. The Index was much quieter than he would have expected, with the rumble of machinery sounding faint and far away, and only a gentle hissing noise from the sparks.

"Hello?" Hugh said. "Index? It's me, Hugh."

Nothing answered.

"Hello?" Hugh tried again. "I made a contract with you through some of your pages?"

Again, no answer.

Alustin finally spoke up again. He looked visibly nervous.

"There's another lie I told to you, Hugh."

Hugh glanced sharply at him.

"The Index isn't alive. It's not sentient to any degree whatsoever- it's merely a mass of information. It was specifically designed, in fact, to not be able to become sentient. Its creators judged it too much of a risk. Instead, it has the ability to be linked to a single, powerful mind at a time, which has the ability to direct it and lend it a limited degree of intelligence."

Hugh gaped at him.

"What... what are you saying, sir?"

The haze was thinning around them as they sank through the Index.

"You didn't form a contract with the Index, Hugh. You formed a contract with the mind controlling the Index. You pacted with High Librarian Kanderon Crux."

CHAPTER TWENTY

The Heart of the Library

Hugh was still gaping at Alustin in shock when they burst out of the mist (and midst) of the Index. He looked around to see Kanderon Crux waiting for them. She rested atop a massive floating dais made of blue crystal. Hugh couldn't see anything below her dais but darkness and mist like that in the Index, but without the glow of the Index's machinery. Her face was that of a stern woman in middle age as she glanced up from the book she was reading.

Said face was taller than Hugh.

Kanderon Crux was a sphinx, with the face of a woman, the body of a lion, and the wings of an eagle. She was at least seventy-five feet long, not counting the length of her tail, and had proportions similar to, albeit thicker limbed, than those of an actual lion. Her coat was a deep tawny amber, and her eyes were a deep blue.

Her wings were what immediately drew attention, however. Unlike every illustration of sphinxes that Hugh had ever seen, her wings weren't covered with feathers, or even made of flesh and blood- they were solid crystal. They were a shade of blue that closely resembled the blue of the Index's machinery, but that somehow possessed immensely deeper depths. The crystals were cunningly… crafted? Grown? However they were put together, they flexed and moved like true wings, with a faint whisper of musical chimes whenever the crystals brushed against one another.

Though the wings were folded up, Hugh was sure they

must have a wingspan wider than Kanderon Crux's body was long. They must weigh more than the rest of her combined. No, more than all the buildings in Hugh's home village.

Their platform slowly pulled alongside Kanderon's immense crystal dais. Kanderon closed her book with a single claw with a loud thud.

Alustin stepped onto the crystal dais, then went down to one knee and lowered his head. Hugh quickly emulated him. The origami pegasus golem that had led them there left, darting back up to the mists of the Index.

"High Librarian," Alustin said.

"Hugh of Emblin."

Kanderon's voice hit him like a ton of bricks, and he almost lost his balance, even lowered to one knee. He felt it resonate inside his mind and mana reservoirs as well.

"My apologies," Kanderon said. This time her voice was much quieter. It was still as loud as you'd expect from a being larger than most houses, and Hugh still felt it resonate inside his mind, but it was bearable now. **"I've never pacted with a warlock before, so much of this is new to me."**

"It's... it's fine, mas... er, High Librarian."

"Master Kanderon will be fine, Hugh."

Hugh finally found the nerve to meet Kanderon's unblinking gaze.

"I am Kanderon Crux, High Librarian of the Grand Library of Skyhold, the Sphinx of Living Crystal, and the last known living Founder of the Academy at Skyhold. I have rejected every single offer to pact with me before this, Hugh. Do you know why I accepted yours?"

Hugh waited for some time before he realized that the

sphinx wasn't merely asking a rhetorical question. He was still a little in shock at hearing her claim to be one of Skyhold's founders- that would make her at least half a millennium old. At least. He shook his head.

"No, Master Kanderon."

"Venture a guess."

Hugh racked his brain frantically.

"Because you didn't want me to contract with Bakori?"

Kanderon snorted, and her exhalation hit Hugh like a strong wind.

"Thwarting that wretched demon is quite a bonus, I must admit. I thought that I'd destroyed him centuries ago, so I was displeased to hear that he survived. But no, that's not the reason, Hugh."

She continued to stare unblinkingly at Hugh.

"Then… why? Why me? I'm nobody special."

A horrifying rasping noise came from deep within Kanderon's throat. Hugh was horrified for a moment until he realized that she was laughing.

"Nobody special, Hugh? You fought off a demon's influence almost single-handedly for most of a year. You attracted the attention of one of my most prized pupils, who I was convinced would never take any students of his own."

Alustin snorted at that.

"You and your friends are learning magical skills that few full mages even attempt. Did Alustin ever tell you how rare your skills are? Only one in a dozen dream attuned mages ever learn to reliably manifest dreams, and of those only a tiny handful ever master dreamfire. Your barbarian friend doing so even with the restrictions of her tattoos in just a few short

months? It should have been impossible. Your little storm mage friend should never have been able to successfully combine mana layering, formless casting, and a truly impractical set of mana channeling techniques. So far as I know, her developing style of magic is unique."

Kanderon leaned closer.

"And you, Hugh. You were so desperate to prove your worth to yourself that you took on a task generally considered to be the domain of archmages. There are plenty of mages who create their own spellforms. Learning to do it on the fly? There are only a handful of mages on the continent with the knack for it. Alustin isn't even capable of it, and had I known what he was up to, I would have forbidden him from trying to teach it to you for fear of catastrophic failure."

Hugh's jaw dropped in shock, and he shot a glance at Alustin, who was avoiding eye contact with Hugh.

"Hugh's skill with wards didn't just come from his warlock related will imbuing talents," Alustin said. "He was an absolute natural at recombining the spellforms that he was given to craft wards with to get new results. It seemed an intuitive enough leap to follow."

"To teach him how to craft new spellforms in a lab, perhaps. On the fly? Sheer ambition on your part."

For all of Kanderon's criticism, Hugh thought he actually detected a hint of pride in her voice.

"So that's why you chose me?" Hugh said. "My ability with spellforms?"

Kanderon's attention returned to Hugh. "Warlocks with comparably impressive abilities have tried to pact with me before, Hugh. Impressiveness alone is not enough for me to pact with someone. No, I only brought that up to make it clear that I would not pact with a nobody, and that I most certainly considered you worthy in that regard."

Hugh looked down at the ground, but a faint smile touched the corners of his mouth.

"No, Hugh, what made me decide to pact with you? It was the fact that you had no idea who I was, what powers I might grant you, or even if the contract would work. You risked everything on the chanciest of bets, and you did it entirely selflessly- not for your own power, but for your friends."

Hugh blushed.

"Actually, uh… I was wondering…"

"Well?"

"What are my affinities? The one I tried to use in the labyrinth was… terrifying."

Kanderon chuckled.

"That is the most offensively oriented of the affinities I've granted to you. It's commonly known as a star affinity, though I prefer stellar affinity as a name. It's closely related to, though distinct from, solar affinities."

Hugh couldn't help but smile and think of Heliothrax, the sun dragon that had been the first entity he'd ever seriously imagined contracting with.

"Once fully attuned to it, you will possess immense destructive capability, but I have to warn you against relying too heavily on it. Spells cast using this affinity are immensely mana intensive, and it will be years before you can use more than a small number of star spells in a day. Even I have to be conservative with their use."

Hugh was a little disappointed by this, but not too much. He'd never even heard of another stellar mage before Kanderon.

"The next should, I hope, be obvious."

Hugh looked at Kanderon blankly, then shook his head.

She sighed loudly. *Very* loudly. **"The second is a crystal affinity, which should have been obvious from my wings, my dais, and the construction of the Index."**

"Crystal affinity?" Hugh said. "Is that to rock affinities like steel affinities are to iron affinities? Just a more focused, powerful version of it?"

"There is… a small amount of validity to that comparison," Kanderon said, **"but it's more incorrect than otherwise. We'll discuss that another time, but for now, suffice it to say that this affinity will be by far the one you use most of your three. It provides numerous defensive options, a few offensive options, and an immense amount of versatile utility spells. It will even provide you with some fascinating new options for your wards."**

Hugh really liked the sound of that.

"The third… the third affinity is complicated. It's closely related to spatial affinities, but is quite distinct."

Hugh had never heard of spatial affinities before. He opened his mouth to ask, but Kanderon pressed onwards.

"It's… sometimes erroneously called a labyrinth affinity, given that it is used in the construction of most labyrinths. I also used it in the construction of this library, and some archmages have been known to use it to create pocket universes. It's also known as a dimensional affinity, but I tend to refer to it as a planar

affinity. The most basic use of it is creating
extradimensional spaces."

Kanderon leaned incredibly close, until her face was
mere feet away. It suddenly occurred to Hugh that while
most of Kanderon's teeth resembled a human's, her fangs
were both much larger and much sharper proportionally.
Her mouth was big enough that she could likely devour
Hugh in a single bite, if she so chose.

**"It is not a natural affinity, and absolutely no one is
born with it. It can normally only be trained. Even
with your exceptional skills, you are never, under any
circumstances, to even tap into that affinity without my
express command. Nine out of ten mages who attempt
to develop a planar attunement die in the attempt, and
I do not intend to waste my effort and have you be one
of them."**

Hugh's heart was racing, and all he could do was nod
mutely in response.

"Why… why is it so dangerous?" Hugh asked.

"Look over the edge of my dais, Hugh," Kanderon
said.

Hugh cautiously walked over to the edge and peered
down into the mists.

"How deep do you think that is, Hugh?"

"I have no idea," Hugh admitted.

**"Nor do I. I originally intended this room to be a
mid-sized addition to a library already lacking in
space, but thanks to unanticipated interactions with
the magic of the labyrinth, this room has continued to
grow every year of its existence. It grows not only when
we add new books, but grows on its own, adding books
seemingly on its own, books that, so far as we can tell,
don't come from our world. Planar magic is**

terrifyingly difficult and seldom works as intended."

Kanderon stared at him searchingly for a moment, then eased back away from Hugh again.

"Will I gain any other magical abilities from our contract other than the affinities?" Hugh asked.

Kanderon raised an eyebrow at Hugh. **"Perhaps, but if that occurs it will likely take quite some time. We'll discuss your duties and training in more detail later, but there's more we need to discuss today. Alustin, if you would bring out the stone?"**

Alustin pulled something out of his pocket. Hugh immediately recognized it as the stone he'd found on the skeleton in the labyrinth.

"This, Hugh, is known as a labyrinth stone," Kanderon said. **"The stone itself is naturally occurring, though extremely rare. Most specimens are used for the same purpose- when they spend enough time in a labyrinth, they begin to channel the mana of that labyrinth through them. Eventually, they begin to allow the wielder to navigate the labyrinth more reliably, as well as bestowing other, more obscure powers. And this stone lay down in the labyrinth a long, long time. If that were all, it would be an exceptionally valuable find, and would serve you well in the future. However... you had it on you during our contract, and it somehow bonded to you during the pacting process."**

Alustin tossed Hugh the stone. He caught it and felt a curious sense of warmth from it.

"I mentioned that you might be able to form multiple warlock pacts due to your unusually large mana reservoirs," Alustin said. "I didn't expect you to do so until far in the future, and frankly I have no idea what a pact with a labyrinth stone will do, or whether it riding along another pact will allow it to become intelligent, like other pacted items."

"Nor do I," said Kanderon, **"which is not a feeling I particularly enjoy. We will be observing this stone carefully. It would be wrong to take it from you, however, so Alustin will be teaching you the relevant spells for maintaining a pacted item- starting with a spell capable of locating it anywhere."**

Hugh clutched the stone tightly, then tucked it in his beltpouch, next to the scent absorbing stone and the last remaining wardstones.

"Two more things before you go, Hugh. First, do not assume that just because you have broken Bakori's spells upon you, and that because I have pacted with you, that you're entirely safe from him. He will not take your rejection of his deal lightly, and he holds grudges for centuries. Bakori is an exceptionally dangerous foe, and it will be in everyone's best interest to keep you far away from him."

Hugh nodded, suddenly a bit nervous again.

"And the second thing?" Hugh said.

"On your way back, Alustin is going to give you a very, very thorough lecture on the dangers of crafting wards on fast-moving objects without the correct compensatory spellforms. You're exceptionally lucky those stones haven't exploded violently yet in your beltpouch. Throw them off the edge, if you would."

Hugh looked at the wardstones in shock, then gingerly eased them out of the beltpouch and tossed them into the mists below.

"We'll be speaking again soon, Hugh. And a fair word of warning- you'll come to view Alustin as an

John Bierce

easy and undemanding teacher."

Hugh gulped.

Hugh rested his arms on the balcony railing and took a deep breath.

He stood on one of the balconies overlooking the sandship port and the Endless Erg. The sun and breeze felt amazing against his skin- he hadn't realized how much he'd missed having more access to the outdoors than a single window.

A sandship was just pulling out of Skyhold's port. Hugh watched it a bit enviously as sand drakes dodged between its masts.

"We're going to be on one of those soon enough when Alustin takes us on that trip he keeps talking about," Sabae said.

"I know," Hugh said, "but I still can't stand the idea of spending more time than I need to indoors."

Talia snorted and elbowed him in the ribs. "I'd always just figured people from Emblin were just normally that pale, and you avoided going outside so as not to burn."

Hugh rubbed his side ruefully as the others laughed.

"What happened then?" Godrick said.

Hugh had been telling them about the meeting with Kanderon Crux.

"Not much. A little more lecturing, then Alustin led me out of the library."

No one spoke for a long time after that. Hugh found, to his surprise, that the silence felt comfortable, not awkward. If you'd told him a few short months ago that he wouldn't just be a mage, but one apprenticed to a battlemage and bonded to a centuries old sphinx, Hugh would have... well, maybe not laughed, he would have

211

been to shy for that, but at least thought you were crazy.

And if you'd told him that he'd actually have friends of his own? Friends who were not only amazing mages in their own right, but who would actually stand up for and stand with Hugh? Who thought Hugh was worth a damn? He definitely would have thought you were crazy.

Hugh took another deep breath, and slowly let it out.

He could get used to this.

Afterword

Thank you so much for reading Into the Labyrinth! If you enjoyed it, please consider leaving a review online- it would be very much appreciated! If you have any questions or comments, please feel free to contact me via my website, www.johnbierce.com. There, you can also find news about the Mage Errant series, other upcoming works, and random thoughts about fantasy, worldbuilding, and whatever else pops into my mind. The best way to keep updated on new releases is to sign up for my mailing list, which you can also find on my website.

If you're looking for other fans of Mage Errant, you can check out r/MageErrant on Reddit! (Fair warning, there's a lot of spoilers there, so be cautious unless you're caught up with the series!)

I also release monthly Mage Errant short stories on my Patreon, at www.patreon.com/johnbierce.

Cover art by Aaron McConnell.
https://aamcconnell.com/
Colors and design by Lee Moyer.
https://www.leemoyer.com/

In the meantime, if you're looking for more fiction in this vein, I highly recommend the following series, all of which influenced Mage Errant in one way or another:

- Dianna Wynne Jones' *Chronicles of Chrestomanci* series: one of the most brilliant and quirky series by one of fantasy's most brilliant, quirky, and missed novelists.
- Andrew Rowe's *Arcane Ascension* series: *Arcane Ascension* is an absolute blast, following a student mage as he tries to find his brother, long missing in a giant magical spire filled with traps, puzzles, and tests.
- Will Wight's *Cradle* series: High-octane martial arts magic series that goes from humans fist-fighting with a little magic up to martial artists destroying mountain ranges.
- Garth Nix's *Old Kingdom* series: One of the most atmospheric YA series ever written, following the Abhorsens, necromancers whose duty is guarding the border between Life and Death.
- Tamora Pierce's *Protector of the Small* quartet: *Protector of the Small* is possibly my single favorite YA series ever written, follows the second-ever female knight-in-training in the Kingdom of Tortall. (And the first ever to train openly as a girl.)

Made in United States
Troutdale, OR
12/01/2024

25663810R00130